₿⁰ˢ

4⁰⁵   1/05- to ash

DATE DUE   APR 0 3

9-6-03	( )		
6-8-04			
7-8-04			
8-7-04			
GAYLORD			PRINTED IN U.S.A.

The Twilighters

The Twilighters

NOEL M. LOOMIS

Sagebrush
Large Print Westerns

JACKSON COUNTY LIBRARY SERVICES
MEDFORD OREGON 97501

Library of Congress Cataloging-in-Publication Data

Loomis, Noel M.
    The twilighters / Noel M. Loomis
        p.   cm.
ISBN 1-57490-460-4 (alk. paper)
1. Wagon trains—Fiction. 2. Large type books. I. Title.

PS3523.O554 T87 2003
813'.54—dc21   2002154269

Cataloging in Publication Data is available from
the British Library and the National Library of Australia.

Sagebrush Large Print Westerns are published in the United
States and Canada by Thomas T. Beeler, Publisher, PO Box 659,
Hampton Falls, New Hampshire 03844-0659. ISBN 1-57490-460-4

Published in the United Kingdom, Eire, and the Republic of
South Africa by Isis Publishing Ltd, 7 Centremead, Osney
Mead, Oxford OX2 0ES England. ISBN 0-7531-6907-X

Published in Australia and New Zealand by Bolinda Publishing
Pty Ltd, 17 Mohr Street, Tullamarine, Victoria, Australia, 3043
ISBN 1-74030-914-6

Manufactured by Sheridan Books in Chelsea, Michigan.

TO SCOTT MEREDITH
THIS IS ONE HE LIKED

The Twilighters

PREFACE

ONE OF THE MOST LAWLESS AND MOST VIOLENT epochs in United States history occurred in the several years immediately following the purchase of Louisiana from Napoleon by the United States. The purchase became known in New Orleans in June, 1803, and immediately speculation arose concerning Louisiana's western boundary.

France at times had claimed Louisiana extended to the Rio Bravo, or Rio Grande, and with some basis, but Spain had occupied what is now Texas—not with any great enthusiasm but with more intent than the French. Through cession and recessions the boundary had become further confused. At the time of the Louisiana Purchase the United States was more immediately concerned with securing Florida, which was in Spanish hands, to assure outlets for the many southern rivers which emptied into the Gulf of Mexico. On the other hand, Spain had lost her status as a great power; while she hoped to retain Texas, she was not disposed to make an issue of a trifle such as the Texas-Louisiana border.

Thus was established, in 1806, the Neutral Zone, a no-man's-land between what are now the Sabine and the Calcasieu rivers, and from the Gulf of Mexico almost to the Red River. This Neutral Zone lasted until the Adams-Onis treaty in 1821.

As often happens, enterprising individuals had taken advantage of this state of affairs some time before the two governments officially recognized it. As a matter of fact, the old Camino Real between Natchitoches, Louisiana, and Nacogdoches, Texas, had for almost a

1

hundred years supported more contraband traffic than legal traffic, for Louisiana was French and Texas was Spanish. In 1763 Louisiana became Spanish in name, but contraband trade did not lessen, for most Texas settlements were much closer to New Orleans than to Mexico City. In 1800 Louisiana again became French, and pirates and outlaws, sensing the uncertainty of the Sabine area's status, began to drift in and join up with contraband runners and renegade Indians. In 1803, when Louisiana became a part of the United States, Spanish troops at Nacogdoches and United States troops at Natchitoches faced one another across a hundred miles of Sabine wilderness, both sides understandably prudent.

This situation was ideal for outlaws. Cold, hard, and vicious, they set up their own Twilight Zone, the ancestor of the Neutral Zone by at least three years. The Twilight Zone covered more territory than the Neutral Zone did later. Roughly, it extended from the Neches River west of the Sabine to the Calcasieu River east of the Sabine, a total width of about one hundred miles, and a length of about twice that. Here every man made his own law.

Emigration had already developed from the Western Country (Kentucky and Ohio) and now received impetus from the news of the Purchase—for few Westerners had any doubt that Texas would soon be a part of the United States.

The stream of emigrants grew larger, and the violent and lawless men in the Zone not only became highly organized, with spies as far away as distant Nashville, but made few attempts to curb the lust and blood-thirst of individuals. It was piracy in its extreme degree, probably more barbarous than that practiced by most of the notorious brigands of history, for here were distorted men whose avarice, cruelty, and viciousness had caused their expulsion from all civilized parts of the world.

It was indeed a strong-minded man who would dare to cross the Zone in that period. But the United States was filled with strong-minded men, and as a nation it was imbued with a vigor and a restlessness that was to carry the boundary westward for another fifty years and for two thousand miles—the greatest migration of all mankind.

This is the story of one small facet of this migration, as it might have happened. I have taken one liberty with known facts: I have called Wiley Harpe by his right name, although there is evidence that he was known to Samuel Mason, the master gangster of Mississippi Territory, only as John Setton or John Taylor. The Foleys are an imaginary family; Krudenier and his immediate cohorts are likewise fictional; major events are well documented.

The news item from *The Natchitoches Courier* has been composed as nearly as possible in the manner of such items in the newspapers of the 1820's, in respect to reporting, rhetoric, grammar, punctuation, and typography.

It will be some satisfaction to the law-abiding to know that within months after this story takes place, both Samuel Mason and the mad Wiley Harpe had their heads twisted off like butchered hogs—which should have been no matter of astonishment to Wiley Harpe, for his brother, Micajah, had lost his head in the same fashion, five years before in the Kentucky Country. Oddly enough, too, it was Wiley Harpe who decapitated Samuel Mason for a reward of $500.

Noel M. Loomis

February 18, 1954

3

CHAPTER I

IT WAS DRIZZLING IN THE CANEBRAKE. THE CLOUDS were heavy and low. Off toward the southwest, over Natchez, the sky was an unbroken leaden mass. Not even a bullfrog croaked.

Bloody Harpe watched the trail for a moment and then looked to the north through the towering stalks of cane. "It might turn cold," he said without feeling.

Woman Claydon kept his hand over his horse's nose and watched Harpe. Claydon was taller than he looked, for his head was small and his middle was too big, but his forehead, under the shapeless buffalo-wool hat, was high and shiny, and white in the gloom like the belly of a catfish; his eyes were small, black, and sharp. "You reckon we missed 'em?"

Harpe snorted. He was a small man for that country, but heavily built. He never wore a hat, even in wet weather, and his kinky hair came low on a swarthy forehead. Heavy ridges of flesh kept his face in a constant scowl. He had stood there in the drizzle for two hours, and his leather coat was soaking wet across the shoulders. Now he said, "I smell wood smoke."

Claydon looked back at the trail and his eyes glittered. He was not called Woman because of anything feminine about him. "How much longer we goin' to wait?"

Harpe said sourly, "I told you there wasn't no wimmen in this outfit." Harpe wasn't even looking at him. "Why don't you go to Natchez-Under-the-Hill? Wimmen are cheap down there."

Claydon glared at him. Some day Harpe would go too

5

far, and Claydon would slice his throat.

Harpe said in a low voice: "They've got a fire built. They'll dry out their clothes and stay all night." He looked up the trail. "Ride a couple of miles and see if anybody's comin'.'"

Claydon jerked the head of the big gray around and pulled him out onto the trail. The gray's hoofs crunched in the cane. Claydon swung into the rawhide saddle and pushed the horse into a trot. Down here the trail was mostly through cane, and a man could lose it if he took the wrong turn at an opening in the otherwise solid wall of five-inch-thick trunks, but the gray had traveled the Trace many times and knew it better than any man, so Claydon didn't bother to guide the horse but let it have its way.

It traveled steadily for half an hour, and there was no sign of travelers, so at the next camping spot Claydon wheeled around and went back. He found Harpe still standing there, still wet, still scowling.

"Nobody," said Claydon, pulling off the trail. Harpe nodded. "That's good."

"How about Swaney? He might come into Natchez early."

"The mailman?" Harpe scowled more deeply, watching the trail. "This isn't his week." He pulled his blaze-faced horse out of the cane and got on. "Let's take these whipsaw fellers."

"Wait a minute," said Claydon. "How much do I get?"

Harpe stared at him. Harpe was almost a head shorter, but he had a way of not looking up that made him seem taller than he was. "Never but two things on your mind," he said. "Wimmen and 'How much do I get?' Some day," he predicted, "one of them two will be the

6

death of you."

"I just ast about my share."

"Three ways," said Harpe. "One to me, one to you, one to Sam Mason."

"I don't like that third goin' to old Mason."

"You're a fool," Harpe growled. "Mason's spies tip us off when there's a good outfit comin', and Mason furnishes a place to hide out when they get after us. What more do you want?"

"We're the ones run the risk of a bullet in our guts," said Claydon. "Our share oughta be more."

"You don't look like you carry no lead," Harpe said sarcastically. "Now fall in behind me and let's find out what happened to them three whipsawers."

Claydon followed in silence, speculating. Whipsawers were fresh meat. When the rivermen got paid off in New Orleans they wouldn't have enough money to buy a horse apiece to go back up the Natchez Trace to Kentucky, so three men would go in together. Three men, one horse. The first man would ride the horse for two hours, then tie him to a tree and walk on; the other two would come up to the horse, the second man would ride for two hours, then tie the horse and go on. Presently the third man came up and got a two-hour ride. Then they started all over again. That way they made good time and didn't get too tired.

That way also was a help to Sam Mason's gang, for the whipsawers generally carried their money in saddlebags on the horse, and a man could often corner the rider by himself.

They followed the trail for half a mile, and at places it was so narrow that a pair of saddlebags well filled with corn would scrape the cane on either side. Presently Harpe held up his hand, and Claydon stopped the gray.

7

Voices came from a short distance ahead and to the left. First was a lazy Virginia drawl: "I ain't hidin' my money, Jed. I ain't helpless."

"Every man to his own taste. How you comin' with that fire?"

"I think I got her goin'."

The older voice said, "Si, you better hopple the horse and turn him loose on the cane browse."

Branches crackled. "Building a lean-to," Harpe whispered. "Come on."

Claydon's gray followed. They went down the Trace a few hundred yards and came to an opening in the cane. Harpe led the way to a small clearing.

A buckskin-shirted boy, hardly eighteen years old, looked up from a pile of wet twigs that were sending up thick white smoke. "Comp'ny, Jed," he said in a low voice.

Claydon took in the older man, who had laid a small ridgepole between two oaks and was chopping down cane stalks to build a shelter against the rain. He looked up. The wisdom of experience was in his eyes, and Claydon knew he was the one to watch. A quick glance put the third man deeper in the cane, hobbling their only horse, and from the distance Claydon thought he too was a young fellow.

The older man asked quickly, "Where you fellers from?"

"Nashville," said Harpe, swinging his horse to the far side, where the young Virginian working on the fire would be in the middle. Claydon stayed back at the entrance to the clearing.

"Whatta you after?"

"We decided to camp for the night," Harpe said easily, "it bein' such bad weather—and we figgered two

8

men alone wasn't very safe." His black eyes looked at the older man. "They warned us up above we might run into outlaws down here, and we thought five would be safer than two."

"Maybe. Got anything to eat?"

Harpe shook his heavy head. "We got money, though. We can pay for our meal."

The older man seemed to make his decision. "Ain't necessary. We killed a deer this morning and saved the hams. We've got plenty. 'Light."

It was, Claydon saw, a rather grudging invitation, but it was enough. Harpe swung down, his pistol in his belt, a sharp knife in a sheath on his left hip, an equally sharp tomahawk swinging from a rawhide loop on his right hip. "I was scairt you wouldn't want us to camp with you," he said.

Claydon swung down as soon as Harpe was on his feet.

"Heard a lot about this here Harpe," said Harpe, watching the young fellow work at the fire. "Mad Harpe, they call him. A real terror if there ever was one."

Claydon, both hands free, watched Jed, the older man. Jed glanced at Harpe's bare head. The kinky hair and the scowling face should have been a giveaway, but Jed went back to his task of chopping cane.

"You ain't the Harpe gang, are you?" Harpe went on.

"Nope," said Jed. "We came down the river on a floatboat, and we're headed back to Kentucky." He picked up an armload of cane stalks. "My name's Jed," he said, and Claydon knew he still wasn't pleased to have their company.

Harpe glanced at Claydon and then at Jed, and Claydon nodded. It would be his job to take care of Jed

9

when the showdown came. Trouble was, working with Harpe, a man never knew when the showdown would come. Harpe liked to play with them. Or maybe he just didn't like to cook his own meals.

The fire began to show red flame, and Jed turned at the crackling. "Build a big one, Tom," he said. "I want to eat before midnight."

Tom put on small branches, and Wiley Harpe said, "I'll go for wood."

Claydon took the reins of Harpe's horse. "Might as well stake 'em out," Harpe said loudly, "long as these gentlemen made us welcome."

"Better hopple 'em," said Jed, "and turn 'em loose in the cane."

"They had a good feed of corn this morning," Harpe answered. "We don't browse 'em if we can help it, for they both stray."

He went after wood while Claydon tied the horses where they could munch on cane leaves.

Harpe came back with an armful of boughs and two long forked sticks that he sharpened and pressed into the soft ground on opposite sides of the fire. He cut an opening under the tendon above the hock of the deer's leg, and pushed a heavier branch through; then they hung the ham over the fire.

There was admiration in the young boy's voice. "You know how to do these things."

"I ought to. I been fightin' Injuns since I was old enough to pour bullets."

"What kind of Indians?" asked Jed, coming up to the fire.

Harpe glanced at him briefly. "Mingos up along the Great War Path, then Pottawatomies out in Illinois country. Name's John Taylor. This here's my brother,

10

Lud Roberts."

"You two fellers don't look like brothers," Jed said quickly, and frowned. "And if you're brothers, why have you got different names?"

"We're half-brothers," Harpe said, and for a moment Claydon thought his scowl was one of sardonic amusement—only, Harpe was never amused at anything. You couldn't afford to be, in this business. In fact, old Mason was the only outlaw Claydon had ever seen that could really laugh without being drunk. Harpe laid his flat, menacing stare on Jed and asked, "Anything wrong with that?"

"No. No, I reckon not."

But Jed's eyes were sharp as he glanced from Harpe to Claydon. The man was suspicious. Claydon would have favored doing the job right away, but he waited. Harpe would kill him and gut him and stuff him full of rocks if he interfered.

They sat around the fire. The third man came up and put on coffee in a tin can. Claydon, squatting, stayed back a little so that he could keep an eye on them all. The deer ham began to swell with juice that dripped down and sizzled in the fire, while Harpe went after more wood, and Claydon stayed where he was.

Harpe got a flat bottle of rye out of his saddlebag and passed it around. When it was empty he got another.

Claydon watched. The two younger men, on empty stomachs, got silly. The older man, like Harpe and Claydon himself, never batted an eye.

When the two bottles were empty, they began to work on the deer ham. It was little more than warm, but Harpe liked it that way—and so, apparently, did the others. Harpe cut off long slices and swallowed them practically without chewing. After a while the ham was

11

gone and the coffee can was dry. Harpe nodded to Claydon; he got up with his tin cup and went to his saddle. Jed said, "You better get that hunting shirt off and let it dry."

Claydon watched. Harpe half turned, the tomahawk swinging from his belt, and said carelessly, "It don't bother me." He tied the cup to a rawhide whang and came back. Claydon had moved away from the fire. Jed seemed to sense something, for now he, too, moved back from the fire to the shelter of the lean-to. His eyes watched Harpe suspiciously. Claydon moved to his own horse and made the motions of going through the wallet tied on behind his saddle.

He left the horse and went deeper into the canebrake. Then he circled, noiselessly. Cane was hard to be quiet in, and Claydon was a big man—bigger than he looked—but he made his way silently around the camp clearing and came up behind Jed in his lean-to shelter.

Harpe was back at the fire. He asked, "You reckon we better put our money in the bushes?"

Jed refused to be led into anything. Claydon, watching the man with his head hunched forward, his eyes on Harpe, felt sure the older man knew what was coming.

Jed said, "Every man to his own likker," and Harpe stared at him. That wasn't what Harpe wanted: he wanted to know where Jed had put his money. It was not an uncommon practice for travelers to stash their money in a tree or a bush away from the campsite in the event of being held up.

Harpe went on, watching Jed's eyes, "Where'd you put yourn?" The man started to his feet. One hand was on the pistol in his belt. Harpe sat where he was, never taking his eyes off Jed.

12

Jed shouted, "You're Harpe! You're Wiley Harpe!" and started to draw his pistol.

Claydon said sharply, "Turn around, Jed."

The older man whirled, his pistol coming out, but Claydon shot him just to the right of the wishbone, and the man never finished raising his arm.

Claydon glanced at the fire. Wiley Harpe—Little Harpe or Mad Harpe or Bloody Harpe—was just easing his tomahawk out of the brain of the Virginia boy. The other one, Si, started to draw his knife, but he was far too slow. There was a crunch, and Harpe's tomahawk cleaved his skull into two equal halves.

Harpe pulled the tomahawk out of the man's head and dropped it through the rawhide loop without wiping the blood off. He saw Claydon coming down from the lean-to, and bent over to feel inside the wallet-like pocket formed by the overlapping of the boy's hunting shirt. He came out with a twist of tobacco and a small box that held a heart-shaped golden locket. He swore, and threw the locket into the cane. He put the tobacco into his own shirt and opened the boy's bullet pouch. He found a small handful of gold coins and some silver. He snorted and went to the other boy. This time he got a twist of tobacco and one gold coin. Harpe scowled at Claydon. "Did you kill that damn' fool?"

"I wasn't shootin' for fun," said Claydon.

"Find out if he's dead. He's the one had the money, I'll lay, and he hid it in the bushes."

Claydon stretched the man out on his back. He listened for a heartbeat but heard none. "He's dead," he told Harpe, and began to search the man.

There was no money on the body, and Claydon grunted and kicked the dead man in the ribs.

"We got a good horse, anyway," said Harpe. "We can

13

sell that to Glass in Natchez."

"Glass don't give us nothing for our stuff."

"He knows he don't have to."

Claydon looked at the three bodies. "All this work for nothin', then. Unless we find where the old guy hid his money."

Bloody Harpe looked around the clearing, studying the cane. "It don't seem to me like there's much chance," he said.

Claydon said, "We could search."

Harpe studied him. "You're a hog," he told him.

Claydon frowned. Harpe never seemed to care very much about the booty. Claydon pondered this as they beat through the cane, looking for the old man's wallet. Harpe was one of the bloodiest killers in a bloody country, but the money seemed almost like an annoyance to him. He liked women and whisky well enough, but he was satisfied to take them as they came. Apparently he did not, like Claydon, ever consider what he could do with a few hundred or a few thousand dollars ahead. The great cities of the West Indies— Havana, Mexico, Acapulco—would be at the command of a man with money. And so would their women.

Claydon stopped for a moment but heard no sound. Harpe had already quit looking. But Claydon beat deeper into the wet cane, his small black eyes gleaming as he visualized the power of that money in those exotic cities. He'd heard that Acapulco was better than Natchez, and certainly Havana, the crossroads of the Indies . . .

His search of the cane was almost feverish for a while. Then presently he began to use his head. The old man, stopped in the clearing, would go just about so far from camp to hide the money. Claydon slowed down,

14

thinking it over. He'd want to hide it close enough so that he could keep his eye on it—and that wouldn't be far, in the drizzle.

Claydon went back to the clearing. Harpe was lying on the wet ground, bareheaded, finishing a bottle of peach brandy. "Better have some," he said. "There's another bottle in the saddlebags."

Claydon shook his head. He stood in the center of the clearing, with Harpe's downcast countenance on him, and turned clear around, mentally calculating the circle that would mark the outer limit of the old man's hidden wallet.

"Whatta you so greedy about? This old man never had any money. They used it all to buy the horse."

Claydon mumbled, "Sam Mason won't like it if we don't bring back nothing but a horse."

Harpe said dourly, "We ain't responsible for what old Mason likes."

But Claydon went back into the cane. Harpe didn't think there had been any money in the crowd, and would so report to Mason. But Claydon thought differently. The old man didn't look like a boathand; he looked like a farmer who'd been taking a load of stuff to market, and this had been borne out by his caution. If he hadn't had anything, he'd have had no need to be scared. Claydon began to make the circle.

He found it high on a stalk of cane—a rough-sewed rawhide bag, pinned by a knife on the side away from the clearing, at the height of a man's reach.

Claydon, looking up, stopped dead for an instant. Then he went on to the other side of the big stalk, and, in going around it, faced the clearing. At that point he could not see Harpe or the saddles or anything else that was on the ground.

15

To make sure, he went on a few feet until he could see the clearing better. Harpe was still lying in the drizzle, finishing the brandy, and Claydon silently expelled a deep breath. Then he went back.

He had guessed right. The bag was heavy with gold—at least a thousand pesos. He handled it quietly so as not to clink the coins. He reached high on a stalk of cane some four inches thick. He cut a vertical strip out of one joint, then with his long, tapered fingers put the quadruple-piaster gold pieces inside one at a time, holding them on edge to get them through the slit, then turning them crosswise and stacking them up inside the hollow joint, thus leaving them above eye level in a living stalk of cane.

He had been careful to make the sounds of a man traveling through the cane. Now he went quietly out another forty feet, sliced off the bottom of the wallet, and pinned the rest to another stalk of cane. If found, it would seem that somebody else had been there first. At any event, it would provide a landmark. Then he finished his circuit of the clearing and finally went back.

Harpe was on his feet. "Thought maybe you was lost. That cane all looks alike."

Claydon nodded, watching Harpe. He didn't think the man suspected, but with Harpe it was suicide to take a chance. "What'll we tell Mason?" he asked.

Harpe shrugged. "We found these three, but they had hid their money. We took the horse to Glass and sold it, and we take that money to Mason."

"What if he thinks they had more money?"

"There's six hundred mile of wilderness between Natchez and Louisville," Harpe said. "Even old Mason don't know everything." He squinted at the horse. "Twenty dollars from Glass—five or six from the two

16

young fellers."

His knife was in his hand. "Get busy, now. We got to cut up these bodies."

"Whyn't we leave 'em?"

"We don't dare. Tomorrow there'd be buzzards, and people see buzzards. Then they'd find bodies, and the next thing you know there'd be a posse." He bent over a body. "We got to cut up the bodies and put them in the bayou. The alligators will take care of them then."

"Why not toss 'em in the way they are?"

"Take too long to get rid of 'em. An alligator likes a piece he can swallow whole."

CHAPTER II

WHILE BLOODY HARPE AND WOMAN CLAYDON WERE cutting up the three bodies, there was activity of a different kind six hundred miles northeast, near the Falls of Louisville on the Ohio River. Kentucky, known popularly as the Western Country—for it was the frontier of the United States—had been in a turmoil of political opinions. It was cold, too, that day in Kentucky, though there was no rain. The clouds across the river were low and threatening, and the wind sweeping down from the lakes through the forests of maple and hickory, black and white walnut and pawpaw, was unseasonably frigid.

At Farnum's Tavern, about halfway between Louisville and Frankfort where a crossroad took off southeast for Greenville, a good many of the settlers were discussing the weather over potions of Monongahela rye.

"Good thing we got our corn snapped before this set in," a farmer in faded jeans pronounced. He emphasized his words by emptying the cup and slamming it down on the rough wood table so that it rang with a dull, tinny sound.

Bill Brandon, a big man with a red nose, filled the cup from an earthenware jug. "The economy of this country is all wrong anyhow," he said. "Here we sit drinkin' rye whisky that has to be shipped down from Pennsylvania while we got corn to burn. We can't ship corn over the Alleghenies to compete with Eastern corn, so whyn't somebody figure out how to make whisky out of corn?"

18

"That there would be a right smart idea," said Jim Sigler, a lanky whiskered man in a ragged buckskin hunting shirt. "It would be a powerful lot cheaper to send three, four gallon of whisky across the mountains by ox team than it would be a bushel of corn."

"That there," said Elisha Wilson, the man with the tin cup, "is why I been fightin' for free rights on the Mississippi."

Brandon chuckled. "You got to find another drum to beat now. The U.S. has boughten Louisiana from Buonaparte, so the Mississippi is ourn. We can ship as we please, and the Spaniards be damned!"

The whiskered man said, "I was shore glad to hear that. I never liked this talk of Kentucky secedin' and settin' up a separate nation. I'm glad it's settled."

Brandon leaned over and said in a husky whisper, "There's some won't consider it settled."

Sigler looked in the direction of Brandon's eyes, toward the big fireplace, where a tall, rather young man stood with his back to the wall beside the fireplace and nursed a tin cup.

The farmer in the faded jumper took a gulp from his tin cup. "No need to pick on Nathan Price. He's a nice young feller."

"Nothin' agin him," said Bill Brandon, "but he married a Foley."

"Don't blame him," said Wilson. "Woulda married Sary myself if I hadn't had the old woman and eight kids—with one under the ground." He went on, musing, "Sary was allus kind of a dream to me, with that long hair like corn silks and them blue eyes that never smiled at anybody but the one she wanted to smile at, and them cheeks that dimpled when she did smile."

"You're drunk," said Brandon.

19

"No, I ain't." He reached for the handle of the cup but hit the rim instead, and spilled whisky over the table.

The whiskered man, Jim Sigler, watched Wilson as he floundered up from the table. The steady drop-drop of whisky on the floor could be heard for a moment. "Hell of a waste," he remarked.

But Bill Brandon was earnest. His jowls quivered as he leaned over the table. "Anybody that marries a Foley has to be a Foley no matter what his name is. Old Mat Foley runs the whole outfit. You get in bed with one of his girls, you vote the way Mat Foley says."

Nathan frowned and stared into the fireplace, pretending not to hear. He was trying to ignore this talk, but it was getting him riled—perhaps the more so because he had already tangled with Mat Foley several times in the six months he had been married to Sarah, and never once had he come off the winner. What made it worse was that Sarah was everything a wife was supposed to be, in bed or out. He frowned again. He had never, of course, told anybody *that*, but it made the domination of old Mat Foley more difficult.

Ordinarily Nathan would have told off a man like Mat Foley, and would then have picked up his family and got out of the country. It was a big West and getting bigger, it seemed, with every mail from the East. That's what a man would have done ordinarily, but with Mat Foley's iron hand over everything it wasn't so easy. He remembered, standing there and staring at old man Fairfax waiting on a young farmer from over toward Frankfort, how pleased he had been when Sarah had first told him her father was giving them a hundred acres of his best land as a wedding present.

He hadn't realized what a whip that would turn out to be in Mat Foley's hands, for Sarah, brought up in her father's ways, apparently thought nothing of his continuing domination after her marriage. Nathan felt glum as he watched old man Fairfax trying to measure out ten yards of calico. Fairfax could hardly see to measure, with or without his square glasses. The young farmer must have been feeling pretty prosperous. Nathan finished his whisky with his shoulders against the log wall.

The three men were still talking at the table, but Nathan closed his ears. What about him and Sarah? How could a man break loose from Mat Foley? Sarah was a mighty sweet girl and she was four months pregnant; he couldn't say to her: "A man is entitled to run his own household. Your pa has got to keep his hands off." She wouldn't know what he meant in the first place, and she would point out all the nice things her pa had done for them in the second place. Nathan shook his head. It was a problem.

"I don't figure," Bill Brandon was saying, "that a man had ought to keep talkin' about settin' up an independent country, now that Jefferson has bought us everything we was askin' for."

"Mat Foley is still follerin' Wilkinson," suggested Jim Sigler through his whiskers.

"More likely," said Elisha, "Wilkinson is takin' orders from Mat Foley. You ever know old man Foley to do what anybody else said?"

Nathan Price heaved himself away from the wall. He discovered he was a little drunk, but he walked quite straight to the table and set down his cup. Jim Sigler looked up at him and then tipped the earthenware jug to fill the cup.

"Gents," said Nathan, his legs spread wide so that he wouldn't weave, "I don't think you have any business

21

talkin' about a man when you don't know what he's countin' on. The news about Louisiana only got here last week. Maybe Mat Foley will change his mind about some things."

Bill Brandon looked up at him. "You know better than that. Mat Foley never changed his mind about anything."

Nathan started to retort but thought better of it. Mat Foley *didn't* change his mind. If he had argued for setting up a separate nation forty years ago, he'd be arguing for it forty years from now. Nobody but a fool would deny that.

The other three obviously took it for granted that Nathan would figure out that answer, for they didn't look at him any more.

The heavy outer door opened, and a small, wiry, black-mustached man came in.

"Morning, Fred," said Bill Brandon from the depths of his cup.

Fred Evans was the editor of the *Crossroads Gazette*. "Gents!" he said. He bounced over to the fireplace, rubbed his hands briskly, came back to the table and accepted a cup of whisky. "Just talked to an ox freighter from the Falls," he announced. "He says the river is swarmin' with flatboats of every description."

"Most likely they're gettin' in a hurry. We ain't got possession of Louisiana yet," said Elisha.

"What difference does that make? Do you think the Spanish will interfere with Kentucky trade now? They won't dare!"

"Gents," Evans said, "I'm proud of Thomas Jefferson, proud of the *Gazette*, and proud of myself for supporting Jefferson all the way through."

"You weren't no damned Federalist. That's for sure,"

said Brandon.

"I wasn't a separationist, either. I believe in the Union and I always have. This country is too big to go splitting up into a lot of little countries. We can be the greatest country in the world if we stick together."

Brandon watched Evans drink half of the cupful. "There ain't all of us feel that way," he said, inclining his head toward Nathan across the table.

Evans looked up, the motion of his head quick and birdlike. "Him? I knowed Nathan back in Knoxville. He's no separationist. He wasn't raised that way."

Elisha Wilson said with finality, "He's a Foley now."

"Never was a Price without his own mind," said Evans. "Isn't it so, Nate?"

Nathan opened his mouth, studying his cup. He closed his mouth again, trying to find the words he wanted to say. After all, Mat Foley was Sarah's father.

Evans watched his hesitation. Then he finished his cup and his eyes were thoughtful. "Tell you something, Nate. You've got to get rid of Mat Foley's hold or you'll never be a free man again. You've got to speak up for yourself."

"How can he?" asked Sigler. "He married Mat's prettiest girl and he's living on a hundred acres of Mat's land. Can a man afford to have ideas of his own in a place like that?"

"The need for initiative," said Evans, "is all the more urgent under the circumstances. Don't you agree, Nate?"

"I say he'll never be a man ontil he cuts loose from the old man," Brandon said loudly. "If he stays, he'll wind up like Mat's wife—poor old soul!"

Nate was instantly resentful. He knew what Brandon meant; Nate had never heard Sarah's mother speak to

23

Mat unless he spoke to her first. But Nate had to say something. "A man's private life is his own business," he argued.

"Nobody has any private life around Mat Foley," said Brandon. The door opened again. This time it swung back against the log wall with a crash that shook dirt down from the roof. A big man stood in the middle of the doorway. He was as tall as Nate and much heavier, with bushy red eyebrows. His red hair was grizzled, but he was in the full flesh of maturity, and he looked like a man who could trot from the Falls to Knoxville and halfway back and still whip the two best men in the county. "Who called my name?" he demanded, and his heavy voice seemed to roll through the tavern, to reach into every corner and behind every obstruction, until, Nathan thought foolishly, nothing and nobody could hide from it. That was the way Mat Foley affected all men.

Evans looked at his cup and found it empty. He set it down, with his eyes averted. "We were talking about the Purchase," he said.

Mat Foley came inside and closed the door. From ten feet away he dominated the group with his vigor and his over-riding assumption of authority.

"What about Louisiana?"

"Lot of boats coming down the Ohio," said Evans. "Be a lot more in the spring."

Mat Foley said: "It's a dirty trick of Jefferson's. He did it to make slaves out of free men. He threw you a few scraps so you'd quit howling for a meal."

Such was the vehemence of the man that even those around the table, Nathan noted, were temporarily squelched. But whiskery old Jim Sigler finally got his bleary blue eyes fixed on the big man. "You don't deny he bought it, do you?"

"Sure, he bought it—and who'll pay for it? Not Thomas Jefferson!"

"You don't buy things without paying," said Sigler.

"In this case we will pay with freedom," Mat Foley said.

"Now look, Mat—" said Brandon.

"Look, hell! You look at me! Jefferson knew we were about ready to set up a republic in Kentucky. That's why he bought Louisiana. Who'd want all that land anyway? It's no good and never will be—and you all know that. How far does it go? Tell me that! Far enough to get us in a war with the British or the Spanish, I'll say."

"Mr. Foley," said Evans, "are you against the Purchase?"

"I'm against it when it is bought with the freedom of human beings."

"Meaning what?"

"Jefferson knew we had twenty thousand men in Kentucky ready to march on New Orleans and take it away from the Spanish. He was smart enough to see that the Western Country might get to be a more powerful nation than the United States. So he bought Louisiana out from under us."

Elisha Wilson said cautiously: "I think you're stretchin' things, Mat. Jefferson is tryin' to do for the good of the country, best he can.

Mat Foley picked up one of the empty tin cups. He poured it full and drank it down, then tossed the cup back on the table. "You can sit here like a bunch of whipped pups if you want, but I can assure you that nobody of my blood will submit to such bribery."

"Bribery?" asked Evans.

25

"What else is it?" Foley demanded. "It looks like sound business to me."

"Business!" Foley roared. "To pay $15,000,000 for land that nobody's ever seen?"

"It settled the question of the right of deposit at New Orleans, didn't it?"

"A few hundred Kentucky rifles would have settled it for fifteen *thousand* dollars," said Mat Foley.

If Nathan had hoped Mat Foley would cool down, he was disappointed, for Bill Brandon committed the error no sober man ever committed with Mat Foley. He asked, "Well, what are you aimin' to do about it?"

"Do!" roared Mat, and Nathan did not know whether Mat had already considered this or not. If not, he made up his mind mighty fast. "I'm gettin' out of the Kentucky Country," he said. "I'm goin' to a country where a man can run his own affairs, where some silk stocking in the East don't tell you where to pay your taxes."

"Where might that be?" asked Evans.

Mat glared at him. "New Spain!" he roared. "Tejas!"

Elisha Wilson looked up. "You'd go to Tejas, to live under the Spanish king?"

Mat Foley said: "In Tejas you can get a grant as big as the state of Kentucky. You can run it to suit yourself. You pay your taxes and they let you be."

"There's still Indians down there—Apaches and Comanches."

"I came here fightin' Indians—Delawares and Piankashaws. We whupped 'em. We can whup these." He looked full at Nathan, his eyes expectant and demanding. "Cain't we, Nate?"

Nathan looked up. He started to answer but changed his mind. Somehow it wasn't easy to answer Mat Foley unless you said what he wanted you to say. While he was trying to figure out an answer, Mat turned back to the rest of them. "You see what I tell you," he said triumphantly. "The eight families of us can whip any Indians on the continent. We hang together, us Foleys. That's why we're unbeatable." He turned back to the door. "Come on, Nate, let's go round up the tribe."

Nate set his cup on the table. He didn't look at the blue eyes of Elisha Wilson, the whiskered face of Jim Sigler, the contempt of Bill Brandon. As he turned to the door, however, he could not avoid Fred Evans's skeptical stare. He met it for a moment, then ducked his head and followed Mat Foley out. But before he closed the door he heard Bill Brandon say to Evans: "I thought you knew him back in Knoxville. I thought he had some guts in him."

CHAPTER III

NATHAN LOOKED UP ONCE AT MAT FOLEY'S BACK. THE
man always seemed to know exactly what he wanted to
do and he always seemed to be doing it without a
possibility of hesitation; it was hard to interpose a word
with such a man. If he had hesitated or given any
indication of unsureness—but he didn't. He strode out
purposefully to the hitch rack, flipped the reins from
around the peeled pole with a single movement that
seemed indicative of an energy that could not be
opposed. He swung into the saddle of the black stallion
and wheeled it away.

Nate mounted his own bay gelding more slowly, but
he followed the big straight figure of Mat Foley. There
was no denying that old Mat—who wasn't really old,
being under fifty—had more energy and purpose in him
than half a dozen ordinary men, but wasn't it time he
was slowing down enough to look around and see that
other people had their own ways to go?

No—Nathan shook his head—to Mat Foley there
never had been and never would be but one way to go:
his. Maybe Bill Brandon had been right when he had
said: "You marry a Foley girl, you're a Foley. You
might as well change your name to hers." So Nathan
Price rode slowly, following Mat, and it struck him that
nobody ever rode alongside Mat; they always followed.
They took the Orsonville road for half an hour, Mat
Foley still ahead, riding with his thoughts—or, perhaps,
with his determination. By this time Nathan had thought
of something to say, but now, as he looked at the square
shoulders of the man on the black stallion, the things he

28

had to say seemed childish and without point.

Another hour, and they were riding a high ridge wooded with locust, sassafras, and hickory. Here the wild grapevines were abundant, but the grapes had long since dried on the vine. Then they dropped down into the valley—the State of Foley, some called it in town.

It was as near to a kingdom as might exist in America (where titles had been abolished), with more than three thousand acres of meadow and grain land. In the meadow the bluegrass grew long and succulent. On the higher ground, where the spring-fed stream did not overflow in the spring, was rich corn land. Mat Foley had a way with the soil as he had a way with people; he raised oats and barley and wheat and rye and flax, and near his home place, at the very entrance to the valley, was a fine grove of bearing apple trees.

Mat had taken up land in this valley about 1790, and had settled there with three boys growing up and four girls at various ages, the oldest already seventeen but for some reason not yet married, the youngest—Sarah—only three. It wasn't long before Mat had bought out or chased out—it depended on who told it—the other settlers in the valley, and had owned it all himself. The upper end was closed off by a mountain; the bottom end was a narrow pass, and there Mat Foley built his main cabin. As his boys grew up he gave them each an acreage; as his girls got married he settled them on land in the valley. Every acre was choice, and it was only a question of time until the valley was indeed the "State of Foley," for no one could come up the valley past Mat's place without stopping or running the risk of being torn to pieces by his bear dogs. If, on occasion, a stranger wandered into the valley over one of the ridges, following the path Nathan and Mat were on now, he

29

would quickly be escorted to Mat's place, practically under arrest, where Mat would question him before releasing him and warning him out of the valley.

They rode through a field of shocked corn. At the edge, where the bluegrass started, Mat paused to survey his kingdom. He sat back in the saddle, erect, broad-shouldered, regal.

From his big cabin at the lower end of the valley, a wisp of smoke curled in a slow spiral, ascending until it was caught by the wind from over the green mountain at the west. Two men were busy down there in the horse pen. Children were fishing in the stream almost immediately below them; those would be the children of shrill-voiced Nancy, the oldest daughter, and George McGee. There had been those, before Nathan started setting to Sarah, who had wondered aloud if George had married the sharp-tongued Nancy to get his hands on that good land.

Two men and a woman were in the cornfield across the valley; that was Ben Metheny's corn; he had married Margaret, the girl just under Nancy. The entire valley was dotted with cabins—seven Foley cabins and half a dozen for their blacks. From every kitchen came a warm fragrance, for Saturday was baking day in the State of Foley.

The dull explosion of a black powder rifle came faintly from across the valley, and Mat Foley sat rigid, concentrating intently on the source of the sound, wondering, Nathan thought a little melodramatically, what manner of varlet dared to hunt in Foley forests. Movement developed at the edge of the woods, and presently a rider came out with a deer slung over his horse's withers.

Mat Foley swore. "That idiot! I told him not to spoil good deer meat by packing it home!"

Nathan studied the horse. It looked like the calico

30

pony of Timothy Hagans, who had married the third girl, Alice, and who never seemed to do anything right. Mat Foley dug his spurs into the black and started across the meadow at a gallop to intercept the rider.

They cut upstream at a considerable slant. On their side the slope was gradual, which made the meadow wide, while on the far side the rider with the deer had only to walk his horse down a steep hill, and the calico pony was in the creek before they got there. Mat Foley put the black into the shallow water, still at a gallop, and its hoofs threw great sprays of white water ahead of it. Because Nathan dropped behind far enough to avoid getting drenched from the stallion's heels, Mat Foley identified the rider before he did. Nathan's first indication that something was amiss came when Foley pulled up the stallion on its haunches with an oath of astonishment. "Pete Brandon! What the hell are you doing in my valley?"

The boy on the calico was about fourteen, gangling and freckled. He said, "I shot this deer up on the hill there, and I figgered this would be the quickest way home."

"You know whose land you're on?" Mat demanded.

"Sure, but that don't mean—"

"It means that I own every acre of land in the valley, and anybody who comes here without my permission is a trespasser."

Pete eyed him, turning this over in his mind. "Ain't there a public road through?" he asked finally.

"There is not," Mat said. "Where did you shoot that deer?"

"Up on the ridge. It ran down this way about a quarter of a mile before it fell."

"Up on the ridge," said Mat Foley, "is my land too."

Pete swallowed. Nathan could see the boy was getting uncomfortable, but Pete had been raised in this country, and a boy at fourteen wasn't altogether helpless out here. "For God's sake, Mr. Foley, do you own the whole state of Kentucky?"

"I own this valley," Mat Foley said implacably, "and you are a trespasser. You not only killed one of my deer but you had the audacity to bring it across my land and through my yard."

"Your deer! Mr. Foley, are you sure you feel all right?"

The grizzled hairs on the back of Mat Foley's weathered neck began to bristle.

"I never heard of wild deer belonging to anybody but the man that shot 'em," said Pete. "There wasn't no brand on this one."

Mat Foley sat more stiffly in the saddle, if that was possible. "To top it off, you're spoiling good meat. Why didn't you dress that deer before you started down here?"

Nathan saw the speculation in Pete's eyes. The situation was getting beyond the boy. Mat Foley was threatening him in a way that was hard to answer—not in words or even by inflection of his voice, but by his very bigness and squareness and the fact that he was holding the black directly across the path of the boy's calico pony. Pete said, "Well, Mr. Foley, I knew somebody down here would hear the shot, and I wanted to get out in the open before they came lookin' for me. "

"What do you intend to imply by that statement?"

"I ain't implyin' nothin'. I'm tellin' you why I brought this critter down here without gutting it."

Mat Foley said coldly: "You will follow me to my cabin. Nate, you will ride behind him."

"I'd better get on home, Mr. Foley," Nathan said. "I

got some medicine for Sarah."

"It can wait," Mat Foley said, and started off.

Pete Brandon looked puzzled as he watched Foley move away on the black; he looked at Nathan and started to say something, but Nathan shook his head. Pete glanced at his own rifle, now lying across the saddle, and Nathan guessed that he had not reloaded. Twenty years earlier that would have been an error that a man didn't dare to make, for Indians were still on the prowl in Kentucky, but this was 1803 and the state was civilized. The bad Indians now were across the Ohio River, west and northwest. Pete lifted the worn reins, and the calico started out after the stallion. Nathan looked back upstream toward the cabin set at the edge of the mountain. He saw no activity there, but smoke lifted slowly from the chimney, and some fowls, gray at this distance, scratched around the yard. He turned to watch Mat's broad back, straight and uncompromising, and let the bay gelding follow Pete's pony.

He wondered what Mat Foley was up to now— though it wasn't hard to guess. He wanted to send word back to men like Bill Brandon and Fred Evans that he was still running the State of Foley.

They passed Ben Metheny's place, with his four towheaded children playing in the yard, and it was noticeable that the dogs, recognizing the black stallion, did not offer to bark. Mat rode close to the cabin and called out, "Katherine!"

She was an auburn-haired woman, and Nathan remembered her as a girl of enthusiasm and vitality, but four children in five years, plus the worry of a shiftless husband, had left her slack-faced and wispy-haired. There again was an example of Mat Foley's domination. Nathan thought privately that Katherine herself did not

33

object too much to Ben's careless ways, but always there was Mat to please. The corn had to be planted when Mat sent out the word, no matter if Ben was off coon hunting or up the Ohio to trade horses. There was only one thing dependable about Ben: he would always be home long enough to get her pregnant.

And yet, in a manner of speaking, that should have been their own affair—Ben and Katherine's. They might have got along easily with nobody but each other to please.

Katherine looked at Pete Brandon and at Nathan. Her eyes stopped momentarily at the deer. Then she looked back at her father. "What is it, Pa?"

"Where's Ben?"

She hesitated. "He went up to the Falls. He should be back pretty soon."

"Tell him I want to see him as soon as he gets in."

"I'll tell him."

She would tell him, all right, if Ben had actually gone to the Falls and if he got his wagon past Mat's cabin without being stopped (which was doubtful), but Nathan knew one thing better than Mat: Ben Metheny hadn't come home sober in three years. How he got past Mat's bear dogs, Nathan never knew, but he did know that Ben would roll off the seat of the wagon, and more than once Nathan had helped Katherine carry him inside.

Mat looked at the four children, all in unbleached one-piece garments built like sacks and reaching to the ground. "Send Barbara to tell Bert I want him too."

Barbara, now over four years old, looked up at her mother and lit out with a yell. The three smaller children took after her, but the youngest, now just a year old, tripped and fell over his own bare feet. Katherine saw him getting up; then she went back into the house as

34

Mat Foley resumed his way down the road.

"Look here, Mr. Foley," said Pete Brandon, "what are you up to, anyhow?"

Mat Foley didn't look around or give any indication of having heard. The black stallion's crupper rose and fell as he traveled, and the man rose and fell with him.

Peter looked back at Nathan. "What's he up to, Mr. Price?" Nathan shook his head to indicate that whatever it was, it was nothing to worry about. But Pete began to look worried, and Nathan knew why. That broad, formidable back under that black hat had worried better men than Pete.

They rode between the horse pen and the harness shed. Mat's bear dogs came yapping around the house, a full dozen of them, but a word from Mat dispersed them.

Mat got off the black and turned it over to Abraham, the Negro. Pete started to dismount, but Mat stopped him with a curt command. "Stay where you are."

Eliza, the black cook, who had been unsuccessfully courted by Abraham for ten years, raised her strong voice in song as she kneaded the wheat flour for light bread.

"O, wash me whiter than the snow: Lord, I'se coming home."

Nathan stayed on the gelding and watched Eliza work the dough in a big wooden trencher. Eliza always wore a red bandanna on her head; she was buxom and good-looking and as black as the ace of spades—and Nathan liked to hear her sing, for she was one of the few creatures in the Foley valley who refused to be depressed by Mat Foley. Even the crows, they said in town, didn't caw around Foley's place until he gave them permission.

Nathan, sitting there, drew a deep breath. A year

35

before, in all the ignorant assurance of youth, he had heard such talk and had laid it to envy, for he and Sarah were in love, and a man couldn't be practical when he was in love. But now, six months married, Mat Foley's tyranny was very real to him. A peculiar thing, that tyranny. It was made up of little tyrannies and big tyrannies, mostly done in such a manner that they were hard to take exception to. That was particularly true if you were married to his daughter, and it was doubly difficult when all eight families lived in one little valley, with Foleys in every direction and Mat himself guarding the way out.

Nathan gave his head a quick shake. He had to quit thinking those thoughts, for Mat, after all, was Sarah's father, and they had to get along. Maybe it was a mood, he thought, though he'd never had moods before. For that matter, he'd never been married before. In fact, he'd never had a family of his own at all, and maybe that made it hard for him to accept this closely knit relationship. He didn't remember his mother at all, and his father only slightly, for his father's hair had been lifted by one of Cornplanter's braves before Kentucky became a state. Nathan had been without brother or sister, without kin anywhere as far as he knew. He'd been taken under the wing of their neighbors until he was old enough to hire out, and from that time on—well, he hadn't even realized he didn't have a family until he met Sarah.

So now he sat on his horse because he knew Mat expected him to, trying to figure things out.

He was there because he hadn't been able to get Sarah's yellow hair out of his mind—couldn't yet, in fact. But what was Pete Brandon doing here now?

CHAPTER IV

MAT FOLEY WENT INTO THE BIG CABIN AND SLAMMED the door behind him. Nathan glanced at Pete and saw him start to lean forward.

"Better not," said Nathan. "The bear dogs'd be on you in a minute."

Pete stared at him. Pete's freckles stood out now against his paleness. "Why'd he bring me here? What right has he got? What's he aimin' to do?"

"Scare you up a little, most likely. I wouldn't worry too much."

Pete said in a low voice, "Are you puttin' in for me, Mr. Price?"

Nathan considered. "You should have known better than to come through the valley."

"If I'd gone the other way," Pete said, "George McGee or Bert Foley might of put a bullet between my shoulders. I didn't figure I should run."

"You figured right," Nathan said.

They waited. After a moment Pete said, "This deer is startin' to swell up under the sun."

Nathan was troubled but he did not quite know why. Maybe it was the scene that morning at the tavern. Bill Brandon had a lot of influence in this part of Kentucky, and he wasn't going to take it kindly if Mat Foley bothered Pete.

Abraham finished taking the saddle off the black stallion and turned the horse into the pen. Then he went down near the creek and caught an old mare. He put a saddle on her, tied a small rope around her lower jaw for a bridle, and set off up the valley, veering away from the creek to hit Joe Foley's place at the edge of the woods.

"What *are* all these goings-on?" Pete demanded.

Nathan didn't know, but it looked to him as if Mat was getting ready to throw the fear of the Lord into Pete Brandon. He said in a low voice: "Sit steady in the saddle. There's nothing he can do."

Eliza was pinching off big blobs of dough and shaping them into loaves. She was singing loud and clear. Nathan heard hoofs and saw Bert Foley coming down. Bert was built like his father, but smaller; he might have had some of Mat's aggressiveness if he had been allowed to, but now, after thirty years practically under Mat's roof, he was quiet and noncommittal. He had married a redhaired girl named Peggy from the Falls; some said she had worked in a tavern there, and they usually said it with a lifting of the eyebrows that was more damning than any words could have been. Whatever she had been, she knew her place as Bert's wife. Though she was hard-eyed and there was always a trace of cynicism around her mouth, she had gone to the cabin Mat Foley had built and she had made it the neatest place in the valley. She had raised three children, but she seemed satisfied to keep to herself. She received few visitors, and herself made few visits except for a trip to Mat's place once or twice a year. She had never called on Sarah.

Now Bert rode up, glanced at Nathan and Pete and at the deer lying across the calico's withers. Then he tied his horse to an iron weight and went into the house.

Pete turned to watch Joe Foley's place at the edge of the woods.

He saw Abraham ride up in front of the cabin, greeted by a pack of dogs. The front door opened, and the dogs were chased away by Joe's wife, Thelma. Abraham did

38

not alight, but presently Joe came out, jamming on a coonskin cap, and went to the horse pen below the cabin. A few minutes later he was loping toward Mat's place ahead of the Negro.

Pete Brandon's uneasiness was not relieved by all this activity. Now he looked at Nathan appealingly. His voice was low, but he was scared. "What can they do to me for shooting a deer?"

Nathan considered. Legally there wasn't anything Mat could do as far as he knew—but Mat Foley made his own laws. Nathan kept his eyes on Joe Foley, coming across the bluegrass, and said, "I think I'd still refuse to flush."

Joe rode around them. Joe too looked like the old man—coarse red hair, heavy eyebrows, dark, piercing eyes—but Joe, unlike Mat or Bert, had plenty of fat on him. It was typical of Joe that he had been in the cabin when Abraham had ridden up for him. Perhaps Joe had once had his father's drive, but, finding that he couldn't exercise it, he had decided to forget it and take things as they came.

He got off his horse and turned it over to Abraham and went into the house.

As yet there was no sign from inside the house, but now two more riders appeared in the valley. One, from across the creek and a little upstream, would be George McGee. Undoubtedly the prying eyes of Nancy, his wife, had seen the activity around Mat's place. That was one thing about George McGee: you never had to send word to him as long as Nancy was in the valley, for her eyes were as sharp as her tongue—and if she had been blind, Nathan thought, she would have sensed trouble with her nose.

George splashed across the creek, took them in with a

39

sharp glance, dismounted, and went into the house. George and Nancy were raising six children, but it was still a matter of speculation to Nathan that anybody could stand Nancy's acidulous tongue day in and day out, for the whole state of Kentucky.

Tim Hagans came up, diffident and troubled, as he often was by Mat's ways. Tim was a small man, younger than Nathan; he had married Alice, next above Sarah and very much like her. Tim spoke to Nathan. "Morning, Nate."

"Morning, Tim."

Tim looked at Pete and the deer and said, "Hello, Pete." Pete swallowed and said, "Hello, Mr. Hagans."

Tim's forehead wrinkled. Abraham came up to take the reins of his horse, and Tim got down. He was small and slightly built, and walked more slowly and with shorter steps than was expected of a Foley.

Now all the men of the valley were present but Ben Metheny, who probably was off in the woods hunting, and Zer Foley, just under Bert in years but more aggressive and the most likely to fill Mat's shoes. Zer had gone up to Harrodsburg six days before to trade mules and play a few cards, and possibly, Nathan knew, to stay in the cabin of a part-Indian girl whose husband made long trips up to Pittsburgh to buy boatloads of white flour and rye whisky. Zer usually returned on Saturday, but not this early in the day.

Tim Hagans turned in the doorway. "Mat wants you should bring Pete inside," he told Nathan.

Nathan nodded. Pete's face was turned up to him. "Mr. Price, I don't want to go in there."

Nathan handed his reins to Abraham. "What can they do to you but give you a good cussing?"

Pete moistened his lips. "I don't know—but I'm

40

scared. Five of 'em in there now. They didn't need five to give me a cussin'—and anyway I ain't done nothing."

Nate didn't admit it, but he too was beginning to wonder what Mat was driving at. He reached for the reins of the calico, but Pete fooled him. He dug his bare heels into the pony's ribs, pushed the deer off with one hand, and swung his rifle in the other. The calico, startled, crowhopped a couple of times and broke into a hard gallop. In a few seconds Pete was a hundred yards down the road, whomping the calico at every bounce. Chickens squawked and scattered. A pig got up from the mud of the creek, ran into the direct path of the horse, then abruptly reversed ends and went back for the creek, squealing as if it had been stuck.

Mat's big figure was in the door. "What the hell! Abraham! Get the dogs! Sick 'em, sick'em, sick'em! Go *git'im!*"

The entire pack of bear dogs, hearing that call, came boiling out of the various places where they had gone to hunt shade. They took after the calico, yapping and baying. Pete looked back as if he had heard ghosts. Then he bent low over the calico's neck as if he were riding from the Indians.

The calico, however, was no match for the dogs. Within a quarter of a mile the dogs were at the horse's heels, snapping at his tendons. Mat Foley was standing on the hard-packed dirt in front of the cabin, his leathery face grim with satisfaction. Nathan jumped back on his horse and went after Pete. The dogs would cripple the calico in a few minutes. They were killers: that was why Mat Foley kept them.

The calico was crowhopping in a small circle when Nathan got there. The dogs were at its legs and worrying its nose, while Pete Brandon frantically flailed with his bare heels. The calico was limping, with blood streaming down both hind legs.

"Git!" shouted Nathan. "Git!"

The dogs hesitated. It was Mat Foley's familiar dismissal, but they were not accustomed to that voice. Nathan jumped down and began to lay into them with his shoepacks. The dogs yiped and headed back for the cabin.

Pete was near to crying. "They'da killed me, Mr. Price!"

"I told you," said Nathan, "about the dogs. Now let's go back and see what Mat has to say and get it over with."

"I can tell you one thing, Mr. Price. When my dad hears about this, and sees the blood on this pony's fetlocks, there's gonna be hell to pay—and old Mat Foley and all his tribe can't stop it!"

"You may be right," said Nathan. "Let's see what's going to happen."

"All right." The boy turned the calico. "I guess I'm not scared any more. I'm just—kinda weak."

"This will all be over in a minute," Nathan assured him.

They rode back at a walk, and Nathan dismounted deliberately. Then he looked at Mat and saw what he had feared to see there: disappointment. Mat had staged the whole thing to get the boy to run, knowing the dogs would take after him.

Nathan hardened somewhere inside. Mat Foley was his father-in-law, yes, but the man was crazy. If the dogs had got the pony down, they would have torn the boy to pieces if nobody had stopped them. And Mat Foley had not intended to stop them. That was clear from the tightness of his lips as he glanced at Nathan.

42

Nathan walked past him, watching to see that Pete followed. Mat came in and slammed the door. Then he went to the table, poured a tin cup of whisky from the demijohn, and drank it. Nathan looked around at George McGee, sharp-eyed and calculating; Joe Foley, fat and introspective; Tim Hagans, troubled and now confused; and Bert Foley, like Mat but without his fire.

Nathan waited while Mat poured another cup of whisky. When you were in Mat Foley's house, you didn't speak first, but Pete didn't know that. He was standing in the center of the cabin, facing the big fireplace, with its deerskin on each side—one filled with honey, one with bear oil. Pumpkins and strings of dried apple slices hung from the open rafters. Pete Brandon looked at Mat and blurted:

"What are you aimin' to do? You tried to kill me with your dogs. Now what are you after?"

Mat looked at him stonily, as if he didn't see him. "You're in no position to be making demands," he said.

Nathan remained by the door, troubled. Pete stood in the middle of the room, so scared his freckles seemed to be laid against white cloth. Mat Foley sat with his cup of rye. Bert Foley sat at Mat's right, likewise with a cup of rye. Joe, unmistakably a red Foley in spite of his fatness, sat on a hollowed-out section of tree trunk and leaned his back against the logs under the deerskin of honey. Young Tim Hagans, perplexed by all the byplay, sat on the floor near the side door through which they snaked in the big logs for the fire.

Pete looked around at them all. His eyes appealed to Nathan, who shook his head very slightly. Then Pete turned back to Mat and said stoutly: "You're holdin' me here against my will. I got a right to know why."

"Ma," said Mat, "the whisky jug is empty."

43

Mrs. Foley, a small, blank-faced woman (if she'd ever had any spirit, Mat must have taken it out of her in the beginning), arose silently and went outside, across the dog-run to the second big cabin that served as a storehouse. A moment later she carried in the heavy jug and set it on the table, then retired to her rawhide-bottom chair in the corner to watch with eyes that never had had, since Nathan had known her, anything but dull acceptance in them.

Mat took time to work the cork out of the demijohn and pour another cup of rye. Finally he looked up at Pete and said, "I'm going to try you for trespassing on my land."

CHAPTER V

PETE BRANDON LOOKED STARTLED FOR A MOMENT. Then he frowned. "What do you mean, Mr. Foley?"

"You killed a deer on my land and you rode over my land without permission."

"You must be crazy," said Pete. "Nobody in Kentucky has to get permission to ride *anywhere*—long as he doesn't do any damage."

"It's the law," Mat said implacably, "and you violated it. You will have to face trial."

Nathan said, "Where you going to hold this trial, Mat?"

"Right here—today."

"You can't do that. Judge Endicott went to Danville yesterday."

"We don't need judge Endicott."

"At least you'll have to have a justice of the peace. You want me to go after Sidney Morse?"

Mat spoke quickly, his black eyes shiny with warning. "He lives eleven miles the other side of the Crossroads. We haven't got time to wait. There's corn to be snapped, and we may not have good weather very long."

There wasn't any corn to be snapped unless it was Ben Metheny's, and everybody knew it. Nathan began to get his back up. "You can't put this boy on trial yourself. You're not the constituted authority."

Mat glowered at him. "I've got all the authority I need."

"What kind of authority?"

"I saw him trespassing with my own eyes. His rifle

45

had been fired, and he had a dead deer on his horse. What more right do you want?"

Nathan frowned. He didn't quite know how to answer.

"If you're so strong in favor of this kid," Mat Foley said harshly, "I will appoint you counsel for the defense."

"You have no authority to appoint anybody anything," Nathan protested.

"Maybe not at the Crossroads," said Mat. "But on my land I have. A man is king in his own home, isn't he?"

Pete had been looking from one to the other. Now he took a hand. "Suppose you find me guilty of trespassin'," he said. "What can you do to me—take the deer?"

Nathan, watching Mat, didn't like the look in the older man's eyes.

"If you take my horse," Pete went on, "that's horse stealin'—and they hang horse thieves in Kentucky."

"Shut up!" Mat thundered.

"Listen, Mr. Foley." Pete looked around the cabin, trying to find somebody else to side with him. "I don't know what kind of mare's-nest you've got here in this valley, but I'll tell you one thing: if you lay a hand on me, I'll tell my dad, and the law will be after you as sure as shootin'."

"Nobody has any right in this valley but me," said Mat.

"You may think so, Mr. Foley, but you're wrong." Pete wasn't insolent; he was scared, and he was talking truth. "You ain't separate from the State of Kentucky. I've heard this valley called the State of Foley, but it really ain't, and you know it. You got to go by the laws of Kentucky as much as anybody else."

Nathan had never seen Mat so furious. He said to Bert, without looking around: "Take the prisoner to the storeroom. See that he gets something to eat. We'll hold the trial right after dinner."

Bert got up, but Pete still faced Mat, and for a moment Nathan wondered what it was that gave Pete the assurance he seemed to have. The boy was scared, and he had a right to be scared, even though there was nothing Mat could do to him legally; still, he seemed to have reliance on something about which Nathan did not know. Perhaps, Nathan thought, Pete was being realistic. Perhaps he was talking just plain sense when he said Mat was subject to the laws of Kentucky. It was easy to get mixed up, living on Mat Foley's domain, and six months of it was enough to make a man doubt his own senses, but there was no question that Pete Brandon had the right answers. The difficulty was that it interfered with whatever plans Mat had to scare him, and might even push Mat into doing something he hadn't intended to do. Nathan watched Pete led past him. He looked at Mat, sitting by the whisky, and said: "I've got medicine for Sarah. I'll be going on up to the cabin."

"Be back after dinner," Mat growled, "if you want to defend your man."

Nathan stared at him. Surely Mat would not carry through this trial idea. What if he found Pete guilty? What could he do then? Not even Mat Foley would be crazy enough to try to punish him.

Nathan went out. He saw Bert put Pete into the storeroom. He caught Pete's eyes for an instant and then went to the bay gelding. He untied his reins from the iron weight, swung into the saddle, and started off at a trot. The wind, diverted by the mountain at the end of

47

the valley, and held back by the trees on both sides, did not reach to the bottom; the sun was getting warmer, and the chickens back of the kitchen cabin were beginning to scratch and cluck while the rooster preened himself under a big old poplar tree.

Nathan kept to the creek. Joe's place was high up on his left; Tim Hagans's was closer to the creek, a little farther on, and Metheny's was just across the creek still farther on. George McGee's was up near the woods, a quarter of a mile past where the deer had been shot. Beyond them all, high enough to be in the edge of the timber, and less than twenty rods from the yellow rocks out of which the creek flowed in a stream as big as a hogshead, was Nathan and Sarah's place. It wasn't a new cabin, but, like all those in the valley, it was well built, for it had been Mat Foley's first toehold in the valley. Earlier settlers had gone to the lower and more productive lands and broader meadows, but Mat had recognized the strategic importance of the spring and had gone on up there, to spread out later throughout the valley and absorb the other settlers one at a time. Most of them had been bought out. Up at the Crossroads it had been said that Mat had made it hard for them to stay and easy to leave. A story was told of Bill Brandon's brother, Ed Brandon, who had had the place at the other end. Ed's corn, left in the field a few days longer than it should have been because he had cut his foot with an ax, had caught fire one night in a stiff wind and burned to the ground. Ed had sold out cheap after that.

Nathan pulled up in front of his own place, which was snugly built almost under a huge overhanging limestone boulder. Three dogs came yapping around the cabin to meet him. The door opened, and Sarah smiled. He raised his hand, and rode around to the back. He turned the gelding into the pen, took off the saddle and bridle and hung them on the fence. The dogs quieted down. He walked to the creek and lay on his stomach, with his arms on a big stone, and drank from the stream. The bed was lined with watercress, and the water was cool and fresh and tangy. He got up and went back to the house. He pulled the latch string and went in. After the door was fully closed he held out his arms, and Sarah came into them. Her hair was golden and as soft as silk floss. He stroked it gently as he held her. She looked up at him and said, "There's nothing quite as comforting as your arms, Nathan."

"Have a bad morning?"

She smiled. "Breakfast wouldn't stay down."

He stood his rifle in a corner and hung his coonskin cap on a peg. He pulled a small paper sack from the inside of his shirt. "I talked to Mr. Fairfax. He used to be an apothecary. He says there isn't much to be done and it probably will go away in a few weeks. In the meantime, try this hyson tea—very hot," he said.

She opened the sack and looked at the contents wonderingly. "Real tea—from China or somewhere?"

"I guess so." He went to the fireplace and pushed the two ends of the burned log toward the center. "Where's Spot?" he asked.

"She had six puppies about an hour ago."

He watched the sparks fly out and settle down. "I've got to be back at Mat's right after dinner."

She looked up from where she had sat down before the churn. "I heard a shot, and saw everybody going down the valley. Is something wrong?"

He looked at her blue eyes. Sarah was as gentle as the down on a baby chick; she wouldn't understand her father's ways at all. He looked back at the log that was

49

beginning to crackle and smoke. "Bill Brandon's boy shot a deer up on the opposite ridge." He paused. "Mat didn't like it."

"Why do you have to go back after dinner?"

"Mat wants to decide what to do with him."

She said: "There's a deer stew in the kettle. It will be ready in time. Anna's baking bread."

He reached into the cabinet at the side of the fireplace and got a crooked cigar. He lighted it with a burning twig and tossed the twig back into the fire.

Suddenly she looked at him. "How can Mat decide what to do with him? He always made us mind him in everything—but Pete isn't a Foley. Won't there be trouble if he does something to Pete?"

Nathan blew out a cloud of smoke. "Don't know for sure. Mat claims he was trespassing."

She looked worried. "Mat has been getting harder and harder to please lately. I hope you won't let him do anything to get in trouble."

"I'm going to try," Nathan said. "But you know your father. He's pretty determined when he gets set on something."

She started the churn. "I know," she said. "But he's still my father and I don't want to see him hurt."

"I'll do what I can do," Nathan said.

He listened for a moment to the steady chug of the dasher. Then Sarah stopped abruptly. "Nate," she said earnestly, "it's Mother I'm worried about."

He studied her. "Your mother?"

She lifted the churn lid and looked inside, then set it back. "Mother hasn't had an easy life," Sarah said, avoiding his eyes. "If anything happens over this, he'll take it out on her, I'm afraid."

He finished the cigar and went outside. He put a

halter on the gelding and took it to the creek for a drink. He brought it back and poured out a quart of oats.

Nathan was more worried than he had let on to Sarah, for she was having enough trouble as it was. It put him in a bad spot, for Sarah was bound to stick by her father, and yet Nathan knew as well as he knew his name that anybody who fooled with Bill Brandon's kid was headed for trouble. Pete was all the family Brandon had. Pete's mother had been dead for many years.

Nathan hung over the fence while the gelding finished the oats. Then he went inside. Sarah was dishing up the stew, and they ate silently out of wooden trenchers.

Nathan emptied three plates. "You're a good cook, Sarah," he said finally.

She smiled, but he could see that she was worried. He touched her briefly, then went out and saddled the gelding. He rode around the house.

Sarah came out to meet him. "If you can find Ben," she said, "he would help."

He nodded. Keeping out of trouble was Ben Metheny's best—perhaps his only—accomplishment. "I'll go by the place," he said. "Ben wasn't there this morning."

"Likely he was sleeping up on top of the haystack."

Ordinarily he would have laughed. They had a lot of little jokes between them, and they laughed a good deal when they were alone, but all of a sudden he didn't feel like laughing.

He walked the gelding across the creek at the ford, and found Ben running bullets. Ben prophesied that Mat had got too big for his breeches, but he was positive about "not gettin' mixed up in no fights." Nate tried to argue but got nowhere. He finally got on the gelding and went back across the creek.

51

CHAPTER VI

TIM HAGANS RODE WITH HIM ON THE WAY BACK. "D'ye think he means to go through with it?"

"I'm afraid so. Mat has had his own way for a long time now."

"It isn't legal, is it?"

"Not so far as I can see."

Tim was troubled. "Only thing," he said, staring at the big cabin below them: "Mat kinda forgets what's legal—if he wants to do it."

Nathan asked curiously, "Is that what Alice thinks?"

Tim said soberly: "Alice knows him, and she isn't fooled. Alice has got a head on her."

"You're lucky."

Tim glanced sidewise at him. "I never got the idea Sarah was blind, either."

"Sarah isn't. Maybe none of the women are. I don't know. But it isn't the women I'm scared of."

Tim said slowly, "It's the men, then."

"There's Mat and Bert and Joe. The boys will vote with Mat. So will Zer if he gets back in time."

"What about Ben Metheny and George McGee?"

"Ben won't even play a hand. And I think McGee will vote with Mat."

There was silence between them for a moment. Down at the creek, the water was running through a riffle, and up near the edge of the timber the blueflies were buzzing over the blood spilled by the deer Pete Brandon had shot.

"Sure," Tim said finally, "George will look out for himself. It doesn't make much difference to him what's right or wrong."

Nathan studied Tim. "You opened your mouth that time."

Tim, realizing what he had said, looked startled. "I—"

"Don't apologize to me. Everybody knows about George McGee."

Tim seemed relieved to have it turned off. "Where's the rest of them?" he wondered.

"Probably they stayed at Mat's for dinner."

"I'm scared about Pete," said Tim abruptly.

Nathan looked at the buzzards circling high above Mat's cabin—for the dead deer was still lying on the hard-packed ground not over a hundred feet from the front door. "Somebody will have to move that carcass," he said.

"A shame to let good meat go to waste."

At Bert's place, his wife, Peggy, was working out in the yard. "Boiling soap, looks like," said Tim.

Nathan kept his eyes straight ahead. He thought of Tim, riding beside him. There was only a difference of six years between them, but somehow six years at their age seemed a lot, and he felt like a grandfather alongside Tim.

They passed the kitchen cabin, where Eliza was still singing and baking, and the smell of the fresh bread was wonderfully warm and mouth-watering. They rode under the tree and stood up in the stirrups to tie their reins. The bear dogs were yapping, but Mat's deep-barreled "Git!" sent them away, and Nathan and Tim went inside.

Pete Brandon was sitting at the table. Mat's wife was clearing away the dinner things. Mat Foley sat back against the fireplace. The log had been allowed to go out, for now the full heat of the sun was on the cabin and made it warm inside—almost too warm.

George McGee and Joe and Bert Foley sat around. Mat said, "You fellers took your time."

"We had to eat," Nathan said shortly.

"We're ready to proceed. Tim, you sit with these three here as a jury."

Tim seemed about to say something, but apparently decided against it. He went over and sat on a meal gum and leaned back against the wall. He looked a little beaten, Nathan thought.

"I will act as judge," said Mat, "and you, Nathan, since you don't agree with us, will act as counsel for the defense."

Nathan's eyes narrowed a little. So Mat was putting him with the goats before they even got started, the same as he had put Pete Brandon. Nathan faced it: there was no right or wrong with Mat Foley, no question that might be a little of both. There was only Mat's way and the other way. Nathan accepted it. "All right, I'll defend him."

Pete looked up gratefully.

"Will you state the charge?" asked Nathan.

"The charge is trespassing."

"And you are going to act as judge?"

Mat looked at him. Mat's expression was difficult to read. "I'm presiding," he said.

"You have already made up your mind, haven't you, that he is guilty?"

Mat's eyes began to harden. "I caught him."

"That's a legal question," Nathan said. "I am suggesting you disqualify yourself as judge because you have an interest in the case."

"It's my land!"

"All the more reason you have no right to sit in

judgment. If you are going to put this boy on trial, as you say, he is entitled to an impartial judge."

Nathan saw the hate grow in Mat's eyes, and he knew that Mat would always be his enemy. But right now there was much more at stake: the enmity of the whole countryside against the Foleys.

"Further," Nathan said, "I challenge the jurisdiction of this so-called court. There is a regular court for crimes committed in this state, and nobody has a right to set up their own court—nor is there any need to."

He watched Mat, but saw nothing but growing animosity.

"If you are through," Mat said harshly, "we'll get on with the trial.

Tim spoke up diffidently. "I think—"

Mat glowered at him. Tim stopped with his mouth open. Decidedly Tim was not the man to stand up against Mat Foley. Nathan wasn't even sure *he* was, for this would go far deeper than what was happening here today. In how many countless ways would Mat make him feel the pressure of his disapproval? Mat's heavy-handed rule of the valley was not a thing to be taken lightly, and Nathan realized that Mat would never forgive him.

Mat spoke to George McGee, who looked sharp-eyed and calculating; to Joe, who was too fat, and who seemed uninterested in the whole thing; to Bert, quiet, ready to do what Mat said. He ignored Tim Hagans and he ignored Nathan.

"You boys all saw the deer Pete brought in on his horse?"

Heads nodded.

"It was shot on our land. Do you deny that?" he asked Pete.

The boy shook his head.

"I heard the shot," said George McGee, "up on the north ridge. A minute later I saw Pete Brandon ride out of the woods with the deer on his horse."

Mat said smugly to Nathan: "You were with me when we rode down over the south ridge and saw it happen. Any argument?"

"None so far."

"That the deer in the yard?"

"Yes," said Pete.

"The calico your horse?"

"Yes."

"You rode down to the creek, didn't you?"

"Yes."

"Where did you shoot the deer?"

"In the woods at the top of the ridge."

"You knew that was Foley land, didn't you?"

"I never thought about it," said Pete.

"But you knew it was Foley land down at the creek?"

"I s'pose it was."

"You got anything to say?"

"Maybe I have."

"You better be sayin' it, then."

"I never knew you owned the deer in this part of the country," Pete said. "I heard you own everything else up here, but I never knew you owned the deer."

Mat said harshly, "You're not on trial for shooting the deer, but for trespassing."

"It seems to me," said Nathan, "that you're the one who brought up about the deer."

Mat glared at him.

"Furthermore," said Nathan, "I challenge the legality of this proceeding, the jurisdiction of this court, and the competence of the presiding judge."

Mat bristled. "You challenge my competence?"

"From a legal standpoint, yes."

Mat said caustically, "I didn't know you was a member of the bar."

"I'm not," said Nathan, "except as you appointed me to be so."

"Where are you gettin' all this legal talk?"

"My foster father read law at night," Nathan said. "I read the books when he wasn't at them."

"Well." Mat turned to the jury with fine sarcasm. "Now that we have a legal mind in our midst, this throws a different light on the proceedings."

Nathan kept still. Mat Foley never backed down, Nathan remembered. He had only meant to scare him off, but he knew, from the way Mat turned to his "jury," that he had only made him more determined than ever.

"I leave it in the hands of the jury," Mat said. "Are we going to have people riding through our valley at will, shooting our deer, destroying our crops—"

"I object to that," Nathan said. "Nothing has come up about destroying crops."

"It would," said Mat, "if we allowed hunting in the valley."

"I would like to ask a question," said Nathan. He wasn't hopeful, but he thought he might as well be hung for a horse thief as for a chicken thief. "Doesn't the survey of this valley provide a right of way for public travelers?"

Mat began to swell up. "I *own* this valley," he said ominously. "There's no need for a public right of way."

"I asked about the survey," said Nathan quietly.

Mat Foley's wife moved unobtrusively at the other end of the cabin.

Nathan said, "You won't always own it, and it won't always be one piece of ground."

"It will as long as there are Foleys."

"I'm not sure of that—but what I asked was about the survey. When you first came into this valley there were other settlers all along the creek. They had a road up to the spring, didn't they?"

Mat didn't answer.

"Then I don't see how you can deny people the right to use the road."

Mat Foley glared.

"Furthermore," Nathan went on, "it is a historical fact that in Kentucky wild game has always been public property, and a man could shoot a deer anywhere as long as he didn't hurt anybody else's property." Nathan looked directly at Tim, whose eyes were fixed on the floor. "I don't know of anything that has changed that right."

Mat asked, "You ever hear of the right of eminent domain?"

Nathan said cautiously, "Maybe."

"I claim that right in this valley."

Nathan said nothing. He didn't know what the "right of eminent domain" was.

Mat Foley drew a deep breath and turned to Bert. "You'll be foreman of the jury," he said. "Get your jury together and decide on your verdict."

Pete Brandon was biting his lower lip, looking from Nathan to Mat and then at Mat's wife, moving almost noiselessly at the other end of the cabin.

Bert got up. "We'll go outside," he said.

Pete sat still and straight and watched them file out. Mat bit a chew from a carrot of tobacco. His wife was sweeping the puncheon floor of the cabin with a sapling broom. Mat seemed very sure of himself. Nathan got up and went to the door, aware of Mat's eyes on him. He looked out at the four men standing together in the sun, at the bloated deer beyond them. George McGee was doing the talking. This whole thing was preposterous—if you didn't know Mat Foley. And it was even a little preposterous if you *did* know Mat Foley. He went back to the table and sat down by the side of Pete. Neither one of them spoke, nor did Mat. Mat chewed the tobacco almost triumphantly, it seemed to Nathan, and spat into the ashes in the fireplace.

The door opened and the four men filed in. Tim went to his place, keeping his eyes down. The other three sat, and Mat looked at Bert. "Has the jury reached a decision?"

"We have."

"Give it."

"We find the defendant guilty of trespassing in the first degree."

Nathan frowned but kept still. The farce was about to be played out, he saw now. The "jury" had found Pete guilty. The next step was to sentence him, and not even Mat Foley would dare to give anybody a sentence—or would he?

Mat nodded as if he was very pleased, while Nathan waited, taut, beginning to wonder how Mat would back down gracefully. For he had to back down. He could go no further with this.

"You have been found guilty," Mat said, "and I hereby sentence you to receive fifteen lashes on the bare back."

Pete was on his feet. "You ain't whuppin' me!" he shouted. "Nobody ain't whuppin' me!"

"You heard the sentence," Mat said implacably.

Nathan frowned. Then he had a thought that would save the day. "Your honor, I move that sentence be suspended."

Mat looked at him, the hard eyes under the shaggy red brows filled with a virulence Nathan never had seen before. "Your motion is over-ruled," he said. "The sentence will be carried out when the shadow of the buckeye tree reaches the cabin."

CHAPTER VII

"YOU AIN'T WHUPPIN' ME," PETE SAID AGAIN. "I'LL kill the man who lays a rope on me."

Mat said, "You're in no position to make threats."

Nathan went outside and looked at the sun and the shadow of the tree. Within two hours at the most the shadow would touch the cabin.

Bert and Joe Foley brushed by him, taking Pete back to the storeroom. But Pete stopped as they pushed him inside. "You'll pay for this!" he shouted. "You'll pay through the nose! Lefty Evans was up there with me, and when he gets to the Crossroads he'll tell everybody what's going on down here!"

They pushed him inside and pulled the door shut. Bert Foley said: "Better stay put. The dogs are loose."

Nathan stood there a moment. He heard somebody crying, and he knew it was a cry of frustration and anger rather than of hurt. He went back into the cabin. "You hear what he said?" he asked Mat.

Mat bit off another chew. "What?"

"He said Fred Evans's boy was up there with him. You know what that means."

"What?"

"It means that by now the Evans kid is back at the Crossroads telling everybody what has happened."

"He doesn't know what has happened."

"He knows that you brought Pete down here and locked him up, and he probably hung around up on the ridge until after dinner. He'll sure be headin' back home now."

"What if he does?"

61

Nathan said, exasperated, "You'll have the whole damn' country on you.

"Meaning who? Bill Brandon, who's too fat to ride a horse from here to the Crossroads, and Fred Evans, who fights with words." He swung on Nathan. "What do you think I picked this valley for? Eight men with rifles could stand off an army."

"This isn't 1783," Nathan reminded. "This isn't Indian country any more. You'd have the whole State of Kentucky to fight."

But something infernal had gotten into Mat—or it had been there all the time and was just now coming out. "Anybody scared of a little gunpowder," he said, "can take out now."

"Far as I know," Nathan said slowly, "I'm not scared—but I wouldn't leave Sarah anyway, and you know it."

He saw Mat's triumphant glare, and knew he had hit on it. Mat was counting on his feeling for Sarah to hold him in line. And what choice did he have? One thing was sure: he couldn't leave Sarah. Another thing was equally sure: there'd be trouble when Bill Brandon, an old Indian fighter, and Fred Evans, who had served under Gates, got their men together and came up the valley. Bill Brandon might be fat, but he knew the tricks and he had faced too many Indians to be afraid to use them.

He went outside and looked again at the shadow of the tree. He looked at the storeroom and then at his horse, but that was out of the question, for sharp-eyed George McGee sat outside the storeroom with a rifle across his legs. Tim came over to Nathan. "Alice was going up to see Sarah," he said. "Maybe we could take a breather."

"All right."

He looked at the calico, standing patiently in the sun. "I'll water the kid's horse first." He took the calico down to the creek, let it drink, and then brought it back.

Tim was in the saddle, looking solemn. They set off up the valley at a lope. The others stayed at Mat's place.

They slowed down when they got near Nathan's cabin. "You don't think there's any use talking again to Ben, do you?" asked Tim.

"There wasn't any before. There's less now. Ben follows a policy of closing his eyes so nobody can see him. He doesn't want trouble, as Katherine says."

"Do you really think—"

Nathan looked at him sternly. "What would you do if *you* were Pete Brandon's dad?"

They walked their horses into the yard. Nathan told the dogs to "Git!" and they dispersed. They dismounted and went in. Sarah looked at Nathan questioningly. "Coffee's on," she said.

Nathan got a cigar. "Smoke?" he asked Tim.

"Never smoked a cigar," Tim said, "but I'll try."

"Here. Light up gentle-like. Don't breathe the smoke into your lungs or you'll get sick."

"What have they done?" asked Alice.

Nathan looked at her. She was very much like Sarah, with the same golden hair and blue eyes. She'd already had two babies, for she married before Sarah, being four years older than Tim, but it had seemed to work out pretty well. Alice made the decisions.

Nathan finished lighting his cigar. "They sentenced him to fifteen lashes on the bare back," he said finally.

Alice gasped. Sarah stared at Nathan. Tim was lighting the cigar. "Are you going to let them go through with it?" asked Alice.

"It doesn't seem like I've got much to say. I tried to stop it."

Tim said, "I wanted to talk to Bert, but George McGee wouldn't let me."

Nathan said soberly. "Unless Mat is running some kind of bluff—"

"Everybody in the Western Country will hate us," said Alice. "What can we do?" asked Sarah.

"Right now," said Nathan, studying his cigar, "I don't know."

"Where's Zer? If anybody could stop him, it'd be Zer," Alice said.

"Zer is off to Harrodsburg."

They were silent for a moment, knowing what it meant when Zer went to Harrodsburg.

"Does anybody know when he'll be back?" asked Sarah, pouring coffee into tin cups.

Nathan drew on his cigar. "Today sometime."

"And no use to ask Martha," Tim added.

Nathan tried the coffee and found it hot. "I might ride out over the ridge," he said. "Zer comes back that way."

"If anybody could stop it," said Alice again, "Zer could."

Sarah hung the coffeepot back over the fire. "Why don't you try, Nate?"

He looked up at her. She was worried, and he was genuinely concerned. She was a fragile-looking girl, though she could follow a plow as well as the next, but somehow she always made him feel protective—now especially.

"It might be worth a ride over the ridge," he said.

She came around behind him and put her slim hand on his muscular upper arm. "It's worth a try," she said.

He looked up into her eyes and touched her hand.

64

"All right, I'll try." He got up. "You stay," he said to Tim. "I'll be back before the time."

Tim nodded. He looked pretty glum. "Don't worry," Nathan said. "If there's trouble, it'll come fast and be over with. It won't be like Indians."

"It'll come fast," said Alice, "and it'll be over with— but how many will be left to know about it?"

Nathan finished his coffee. "There are no cowards in Kentucky," he stated, "and this is a thing that nobody would be cowardly about." He set down the cup. "I'll be back," he told Tim.

He mounted the gelding and rode across the creek, up the slope on the opposite side halfway between George McGee's and Ben Metheny's. He heard Nancy's never ceasing voice haranguing the six children, and he thought of George. There was a man who expected some day to control Foley's valley. He was a sharp-eyed Yankee, that McGee, but Nathan wondered dryly if George had ever taken Bert and Zer into consideration. In Nathan's private opinion, Bert was no man to fool with. He never said much, but he was a red Foley through and through. And what of Zer Foley, who had somehow managed to preserve a certain amount of independence and still get along with Mat?

George McGee had a long way to go. He was a schemer, all right, but a good strong man like Zer or even a stubborn man like Bert could upset him. Nathan figured privately that Ben Metheny had the better approach; he did as little as possible, just waiting for whatever might come to him. He did nothing to get in bad with anybody. There were times when Nathan wished he could be the same way.

It would be better not to wonder about Zer Foley, for instance. It was no secret that Zer's marriage was a failure, for his wife had been a backwoods beauty and had some hifalutin ideas about circulating in society on the strength of the Foley name. This had not suited Mat, and Zer must have agreed with him. Mat's motivation was obvious; he opposed anything that might encourage outsiders to come to the valley either on business or on pleasure. Zer's motivation might have been different; he was not a man to talk about such things. At any rate, it was noticeable that when Martha got frosty Zer never complained, but began to ignore her. Even among frontier people, who were not always talkative with one another, Zer and Martha's mutual hostility was noticeable. It was lucky, Nathan thought, that they hadn't any children—and probably never would, now, for Ben Metheny said they didn't even sleep together.

He left the valley and rode up into the woods. Here were more hickory and the ornamental sassafras and some maple, and it was a good place for deer because a fire had killed off the small stuff a few years before, and now the growth was crowded with saplings on which deer liked to browse.

He picked up the trail and rode over the ridge. As he understood it, Mat's land extended to the top of the ridge, but he didn't know the exact legal limits. He went down on the other side, a much more gradual slope, and presently came out of the forest and crossed a wide prairie.

He had just reached the woods on the other side and was ready to turn back when he heard a hail, "Nate Price!"

"Ho!" said Nate, and stopped the gelding.

In a moment a black horse appeared from the depths of the woods, and there were the familiar red hair, square shoulders, and straight back that marked a Foley.

Even the horse, except for a white foot, was very much the same as Mat's black stallion. Nathan waited, and Zer pulled up alongside, a short-handled riding whip in his right hand. "Expectin' me?" he asked.

"Yes." Nathan turned the gelding and rode after him along the trail.

"Martha?" asked Zer without emotion.

"No, not Martha." He told Zer what had happened.

Zer pulled back until their horses were even on the prairie. His dark eyes were piercing, but his face and voice were calm, without emotion.

"That's a fool thing to do," he said. "Mat should know that. He can't fight the whole State of Kentucky."

"What I figured," said Nathan. "But he's running a bluff mighty far."

"You pointed that out, I take it."

"As best I could. In fact, I might even have made it worse by opposing him."

"Mat don't like opposition," said Zer thoughtfully, "but there's some things—"

"Opposition or not, if Mat goes through with this—"

"Like as not they'll chase us all out of the valley."

"They couldn't do that, could they?"

"I was in this country ten years before you were," Zer said. "They said we'd never beat the Indians—but we did, with rifles and axes and sharp knives."

"That was a long time ago."

"Not so long. No longer than Mat's kind of justice if he carries through this whipping." Their horses were trotting now. "Trouble is, there's plenty, includin' Bill Brandon, who lived through that period when the law was in a rifle. I think you and Tim are right: if Mat goes through with it, he'll turn loose people who haven't forgotten how they came out here even before Mat did, when there was no judge and no sheriff."

Nathan felt a little relieved. "You don't think we're dreaming up trouble, then?"

"Wish I could," said Zer, "but it sounds to me like bad trouble if Mat lays a hand on the Brandon kid."

They entered the forest, and Nate dropped behind. "D'you reckon—"

"I don't know." Zer shook his head. "Last time I opposed Mat I was twelve years old, and he whaled the tar out of me with a buggy trace. I couldn't sit down for a week." He shook his head. "It damn' sure taught me a lesson. I spent the last twenty-two years avoiding any direct conflict with him—but now, I don't know. It might be the only way. I can't think of anything else right now." They topped the ridge.

"How could they run us out of the valley?"

"Mat could tell you that better than me. A couple of men with rifles on each ridge, fire in the corn, animals run off." He took a deep breath. "If Bill Brandon would take a notion to clean the Foleys out of the valley, we wouldn't last six months—and nobody should know that better than Mat."

"There used to be talk that Mat got control of the valley that way."

Zer shrugged. They rode a little farther and broke out into the open on the north edge of the valley.

Zer seemed to be engaged in deep thought. "I think I better ride down there alone," he said, "and see what I can do. You go after Tim and take your time. Maybe by the time you get there—"

Nathan looked down the valley at the cluster of cabins that marked Mat Foley's place. "Quiet down there," he observed. "Nothing moving but a couple of blacks at Tim's place, scalding a hog, and half a dozen buzzards waitin' for a chance at that deer."

Zer pulled up. His eyes narrowed as he scanned the lower end of the valley. "Too damn' quiet," he said finally. "Didn't you tell me the kid said he was huntin' with Lefty Evans?"

"Yes."

"Then," Zer said slowly, "Lefty has had plenty of time to get to the Crossroads and stir things up." He started the black down the slope. "I never seen things so quiet in the valley."

"Maybe everybody's kind of scared, waitin' to see what Mat is goin' to do with the kid."

"There's that—and somethin' else." Zer Foley stood up in his saddle. "When we come here," he said, "a man had to develop a sort of sixth sense that told when trouble was brewin'. If he didn't, he didn't live long."

"You think it's brewin' now?"

"It's brewin'," Zer said positively. "I got a feeling them hills around Mat's place are full of rifles right now."

"Why don't they come into the open and demand the kid's release?"

Zer Foley swung on him. "Mat's a power," he said. "He may be arbitrary, but he's a power, and men like Brandon and Evans know enough to leave him be until he actually does something. I'd say they're waitin'."

"You think—"

"We done enough thinkin'." Zer whipped the black into a lope. "I'll see you down there," he called back.

"Yes." Nathan spurred the gelding as he reached the flat, and they crossed the stream at a gallop. He turned uphill then and let the gelding have its head, while Zer made tracks for Mat's place.

Tim on his own calico rode out to meet Nathan. He

69

was whitefaced. "It's too late!" he said. "They've started down there already!"

Nathan stood up in his stirrups and looked around. Zer was halfway between Ben Metheny's place and Mat's place, riding hard. Ben and Katherine were standing outside, watching downstream. At Tim's place, a little below Nathan and Tim now, and a little higher on the slope of the meadow, the two blacks were proceeding with their butchering. The hog was hung by its hind legs to the low limb of a gnarled catalpa tree. A fire was burning at one side, and the hard-packed ground was dark in one spot, showing where they had emptied a tub of scalding water. They now had two tubfuls of intestines and were beginning to skin the carcass.

But the activity at Mat's place was the focal point of the valley. Even up at George McGee's place, Nancy was quiet for a change, shading her eyes with her hand as she tried to see what was going on at the lower end of the valley. Nathan looked back. Sarah and Alice also were watching. At Zer's place, up near the woods, even Martha, usually aloof from doings of the red Foleys, was outside, watching Zer's black horse, and ahead of them, but also up at the edge of the woods, Joe Foley's wife, Thelma, was outside, surrounded by her four children, intent on the activities at Mat's place.

Drawing closer, they began to see more clearly what was taking place in front of Mat's cabin.

"They brung him out," said Tim. "Uh-huh."

Joe Foley and George McGee, both in linsey-woolsey hunting shirts, were holding Pete Brandon between them while Mat Foley seemed to be telling them what to do. Pete's hands were tied, and his first high-voiced protests came to them. Zer, about halfway to the cabin, was urging his black to greater speed.

George McGee came out of the kitchen cabin with a wooden tub which he took to the front yard and turned upside down near a big black willow tree. They laid Pete Brandon across the tub and tied his hands to one handle of the tub, his feet to the other. George McGee brought a strap from the storeroom. There was some conference, which ended by Bert's cutting off the end, which probably held a buckle or a spring hasp, with his hunting knife. Pete Brandon wasn't imploring: he wasn't threatening. He was face to face with a whipping and he knew it, and now he kept still and waited, as Kentucky pioneers had kept still before him and waited for Indians' tomahawks or hot irons.

Mat stepped up and ripped Pete's shirt down the middle with his knife, leaving his back bare. Zer was a hundred rods away. He shouted something, but Mat grabbed the strap and laid on the first one. They heard it smack into the boy's flesh.

At almost the same time Mat spun, clutched his left shoulder, and staggered. Then he ran to the south side of the willow tree and shouted, "Take cover!"

McGee ran for the creek bank. Joe and Bert Foley hightailed it to the cabin, while bullets kicked up dirt at their feet.

A twig dropped onto Mat's arm, and at the same time he ducked; then the report of a rifle from the south ridge floated down.

Nathan yelled at Tim: "Zer was right. The place is surrounded!" Mat was standing under the willow, holding his shoulder. Pete Brandon was still strapped to the tub. The strap was on the ground near the dead deer. Zer Foley slid his horse to a stop and jumped off. "They'll kill you for this!" he roared at Mat.

71

Mat looked like a wounded bear about to charge. His hat was off and his shock of grizzled red hair gave him a ferocious appearance, which was emphasized by his heavy eyebrows and the square set of his jaw.

"Nobody shoots me in my own yard," he growled.

Zer stood straight up to him. "You've got no right to whip anybody else's kid."

"He was on my land."

Zer ran over to the boy. With his hunting knife he cut the rawhide thongs that bound Pete's hands and feet. The boy got to his feet, obviously confused. He looked at Zer as if he wondered what new torture was coming his way.

At that moment shots rang out from Mat's cabin. Nathan and Tim pulled up, still ten rods away. They saw bark fly from the logs, and heard the distant reports of rifles from the south ridge.

Mat, without a rifle or a pistol, walked heavily to the cabin, apparently oblivious of the shooting. Zer turned toward the south ridge and held up both hands, palms forward.

Mat stumbled into the cabin. Two more shots came from there. An answering bullet slammed into the wooden tub from the north ridge, raising it up on one side. Pete took one look. His face was white. He saw the tub jump up, and he ran for his horse. Then Mat Foley's bear dogs came raging around the corner of the cabin. Pete jumped into the saddle, and started the calico at a hard gallop. Shots began to pour into the pack from both ridges. Here and there a dog yelped and fell, but the main pack went on after the calico, while answering shots continued to come from the cabin. Zer started running on foot after the dogs. He shouted, "Git!" but the dogs kept after the boy and the horse.

Zer ran for his own black, which had wandered down to the creek. Nathan and Tim held back to keep out of the line of fire.

The dogs gained on the horse and started snapping. Its left leg suddenly bent, and Nathan knew it was hamstrung. The pony tried to stand, but they got its other hind leg and it went down.

Pete fell into the middle of the pack. They swarmed over him, snarling and snapping.

Nathan shouted, "He has no weapon!" and spurred forward. Zer was galloping up from the creek. Shots were coming from all around, and it was hard to tell where anybody was shooting.

The boy was down, smothered under the dogs. He got up, bloody, fighting them off with his hands and feet. Shots poured into the pack of dogs, but they were close, very close, to the boy. Pete, spinning around, trying to beat off the dogs, glanced up at Nathan, terrified.

Nathan was within two rods of him when Pete dropped, not overcome by the dogs, but suddenly, as though hit on the head. Zer rode into the dogs, striking right and left with his whip. "Git!" he shouted hoarsely. "Git!" He smashed a big brindle hound across the back with the loaded end of the whip, and it dropped, its spine broken. The rest of them hesitated, then ran for cover. Zer went to pick up Pete. The firing had stopped. He held Pete in his arms. The boy was strangely limp, and Zer looked puzzled. "He's bitten and scratched," Zer said to Nathan, "but what dropped him?" Nathan shook his head. "They—" He looked up at the south ridge, and then at the house. Instinctively he knew. "Turn him over," he said.

Zer laid him on the ground. Together they turned him over. Across the bare back was the red welt raised by

73

the strap, and just to the left of the backbone was a small black discoloration with a little blood oozing from the center.

"A bullet hole!" Zer whispered. "They shot him!"

He listened for a heartbeat but heard none. He stood up and looked at Nathan.

"*Who* shot him?" asked Nathan.

CHAPTER VIII

HARPE AND CLAYDON TOSSED THE LAST PIECE INTO the brown water of the bayou. The drizzle had stopped, but the clouds were still low and gray. Harpe scowled at the cane, but it seemed to Claydon there was satisfaction in his voice as he said, "It were a bloody business for small pay."

Claydon cleaned his knife on some wet moss. "Where we goin' now?"

Harpe eyed him. "This was too easy, my way of thinkin'—and you ain't satisfied with the money."

"I didn't say—"

"You ain't got enough money to suit your taste. You figger when you get enough money you can buy whatever you want."

"I never said—"

"You don't need to."

Claydon didn't try to answer again. He waited for Harpe to say his piece, but his eyes were watchful.

"We can have some real fun," said Harpe. "We'll go over to the river and wait for a boat. Then we'll get them to pull into shore. Them fellers gener'ly have money," he added.

"Is this a Mason deal?"

Harpe scowled. "How can Mason know about this? He didn't give us the tip."

"How do we divide, then?"

"Halvers," said Harpe.

"All right," said Claydon. He did not look back at the clearing as they rode away.

They camped out in the cane that night, and went on

west the next morning. The sun was shining that day, and Harpe's leather coat gradually dried, though he hadn't taken it off. They didn't stop to eat, and Claydon knew better than to ask, for Harpe thought nothing of going without food for days.

They came out on a high bank overlooking the Mississippi, and followed it south until it shallowed out into a wide draw, the bottom of which was at the edge of the water. Harpe looked the place over and said to Claydon: "We'll ride back a ways and leave our horses and rifles in cover. Keep your pistol and your knife under your shirt." He took the tomahawk out of its loop and thrust it inside his shirt.

"You better know what you're doin'," said Claydon.

"I've done this before," said Harpe. "Let's cache the horses." They went back up the hill and found a place where the horses could browse out of sight of the draw, and there they hobbled both horses, left their rifles at an oak tree, and went back down to the river's edge.

"We've got no skiff," said Claydon. "How do we—"

"Just watch me and keep your mouth shut."

Within an hour three boats came down together, and Harpe pulled Claydon down behind some trumpet-flower vines so that they could not be seen. "There's only two of us. Let's wait for one alone," he whispered.

A while later there were four boats together, and then, not half an hour behind the four, came one. Harpe's dark eyes filled with an odd light when he saw it.

"I make out about four men—maybe five," he said, staring upstream. "A farmer takin' his stuff downriver."

"It's a shame we can't do anything with the cargo," said Claydon, studying the broadhorn.

"Nothin' we can do. Mason would find it out."

"But—"

"Don't pass no talk," Harpe growled. "We'll have our fun while we can. If you and me took a cargo into Natchez we'd be in trouble. We've got no clearance papers, no nothin'. Stick close, I say. Let's have our fun."

Claydon was not sold on passing up the potential wealth represented in the cargo, but he kept still. Best not to cross the man too much. Whatever happened, he was accumulating some nest eggs along the Trace, and when the time came . . .

"Ahoy!" shouted Harpe. "Boat ahoy!"

Claydon stared at him. Harpe had twisted himself into a deformity that for a split second fooled even Claydon. One leg was bent and one foot was dragging, and his head was down on his chest, with his shoulders twisted so that he seemed to be a hunchback. He ran haltingly up and down the short strip of open ground at the edge of the water, crying, "Ahoy! Boat ahoy!"

Claydon, following Harpe's example, clapped a hand to his left side, bent over frontward, and stumbled down toward Harpe.

A husky young fellow, naked to the waist and brown as coffee, was handling the sweep oar of the flatboat. He lifted the oar out of the water, watched Harpe for a moment, and then called over his shoulder, "What'll I do, Pa?"

"Pay him no mind," came the prompt answer. "Hold your course down the middle."

The boat continued to drift, the sweep oar held high. There was some low-voiced talk on board, and around the whisky barrel gathered the crew—four coonskin-capped, stringy, strong-looking fellows, one of whom was taller and older.

Claydon had time to see that Harpe had judged the

angle well. The boat was still above them and had plenty of time to swing into shore. He stood back of Harpe, bent over, holding his side, while Harpe continued his grotesque performance.

"Help! We need help!"

The pilot looked around, but the older man said implacably, "Keep 'er straight, Abner."

Another, higher voice said: "These fellers been hurt, Pa. Maybe they had a brush with outlaws."

Their voices carried clearly across the water, and Claydon watched Harpe. No matter the man's disregard for money and even women, he was a past master at this kind of thing, and Claydon was a man who was willing to learn the tricks of his trade. "We been ambushed by Indians!" Harpe shouted.

"They been hurt!" said the pilot.

"It ain't so far to Natchez," the old man answered. "Git your oar in the water."

"Just a little food," Harpe begged. "We haven't eaten for three days.

"We got plenty of flour and bacon," the high-voiced one said.

The older man didn't sound entirely convinced, but he conceded. "All right, pull in. We'll toss 'em some vittles and be on our way."

"God bless you!" Harpe shouted, and Claydon raised his eyebrows. He'd heard tales that Harpe sometimes impersonated a preacher, but he'd never seen it done before.

The boat turned ponderously. It was a clumsy thing, square-sterned and square-bowed, with the deck planked over flat with the sides. A whisky barrel was in the center of the flat deck, with an upended box near it for card playing. Otherwise, the deck was clear except for a few scattered buffalo robes no doubt used for sleeping. Of course, there was no propelling power. The two- to three-mile current was enough to move them steadily and make a good day's journey, for they wouldn't have to stop until nightfall.

The boat now was within two hundred feet. The pilot heaved mightily on the sweep oar to bring her in. The older man stood spraddle-legged by the whisky barrel. He was dubious, Claydon saw, but apparently there was nothing he could put his finger on. He had probably been warned, but, without experience on the river, he was an easy victim.

Harpe shouted: "You better not bring her in any further! The water's shallow up here."

"He's right, Pa," said a younger voice. "I teched bottom."

Claydon continued to observe everything with his sharp black eyes.

Harpe was wringing his hands as if in pain. "They put you to the fire?" called the old man.

Harpe delayed his answer as a wronged preacher might have delayed, and when he answered his voice was strong and sonorous: "The Choctaw are heathens. They know not what they do or that it is against the law of God. I hold naught against them for it."

The old man was thoroughly convinced now. He made a motion, and one of the boys flung a coil of rope toward shore. Claydon, still holding his side, ran upstream and waded a little way into the water to grasp it. Then he went back to shore and tied it to the base of a sapling. The boat swung in toward shore.

"You-all don't need to git wet," the old man said, his voice more conversational now that the boat was less than forty feet away. "We'll bring you some vittles.

Abner, get a side of bacon and dish up a can of flour. Better throw in a cup of coffee too. It's still two days to Natchez on foot."

Abner left his sweep oar and disappeared below the flat-topped deck.

"These here Choctaws, now—somethin's got to be done about 'em," said the old man. "The damned heathens—er, pardon, Reverend."

Harpe's sonorous voice rolled across the water. "The Lord's will be done, my good man. The benefits of civilization and His holy Word will reach them in time, and then the savages will live in mortal shame of their infamous deeds."

Claydon heard this exchange with considerable admiration for Wiley Harpe's accomplishments. Harpe was now wading into the water toward the boat.

The old man sounded a little uneasy. "We'll bring it to you, Reverend."

"Nay," said Harpe. "It is not necessary for you to run the risk of snakes and alligators."

"Your cuts—"

"These wounds," Harpe proclaimed, "are but badges of service in the Lord."

By this time he had reached the boat, and Claydon was behind him. The water was to mid-thigh. Harpe put his hands on the boat railing and appeared to try to lift himself on board, but fell back.

Two of the young fellows rushed to his aid, and at the same time Claydon was climbing on board a few feet farther down.

Abner came from below the deck with a tow sack half filled. He was indeed a good specimen, Claydon noted, and moved to a position where he would have an opportunity to use his knife swiftly, for he knew from the trend of Harpe's actions that Harpe would take care of the old man.

The tow sack was deposited at Harpe's feet, and Harpe fumbled in the wallet formed by the lap-over of his leather shirt.

"You needn't pay us," the old man said.

"We ask no charity," said Harpe. "We have money."

The old man said suddenly, "Why didn't the Choctaws take your money?"

Harpe fixed his glowering eyes upon the tall man. "The red heathen," he proclaimed, "knows not the sinful power of gold." He gave the old man, who had long stringy mustaches, a gold coin.

"You'd better let us dress your wounds, Reverend," said the high-voiced boy.

"Nay, they are but scratches." Harpe hefted the sack, but then put it back on the deck and said: "I would buy a rifle from you, sir, to pursue our journey. We may encounter these savages again."

The old man worked his mouth. "Well, now, Reverend, we hain't rightly got any extra rifles. We only brung one apiece."

"You have five," Harpe pointed out, "while we have none—and we must travel outlaw-infested trails." He peered up at the old man from his hunchbacked position. "They say that even the mad Harpe is at large in this country."

Claydon could not understand what quirk prompted the man to bring up the subject of himself. It seemed a dangerous thing to do, but it was one of Harpe's favorite tricks.

The old man started shaking his head, but Abner said quickly, "I'll sell him mine, Pa."

"You'll need it when we come back up the Trace,"

the old man growled.

"We can't turn these gents loose to the mercy of the Indians."

"Well, all right. But," he said to Harpe, "you'll have to pay the usual price."

"We'll pay." Harpe brought out more gold pieces. "Would ye say thirty dollars?"

Abner looked pleased. "That's more than—"

"Shut up!" said the old man. "Git the rifle."

Abner lay on his stomach on the deck, reached down through the opening, and brought up the long, small-bored Kentucky rifle. "We'll need a bit of ball and powder," said Harpe. "And will ye load it for us?"

This was done, Abner using a powder flask that hung from the corner of the card table. He put the ramrod back in place in its rings under the barrel, and handed the rifle to Harpe.

"It's all ready to shoot?" Harpe asked.

"All ready."

"The flint's in place and the striker's in good condition?"

"Sure," said the old man. "I guess you haven't used firearms very much, Reverend."

Claydon edged nearer Abner. A slight breeze had sprung up from shore to riffle the water, and the boat, swinging against the muddy bottom, began to rock a little.

"Not much," said Harpe, holding the rifle aimed at the old man's chest. "You pull this thing here?"

"Hey—no!" The old man started toward him, but Harpe pulled the trigger. The old man staggered, and through the cloud of black powder smoke his face showed amazement.

But there was no time to watch him. Claydon had

work to do. He drove his knife into Abner's heart, holding the blade flat side up so that it would slip between the ribs. Harpe dropped the rifle and slid the tomahawk out of his shirt. He cleaved one skull and turned to a second man, but the third was closing on him from the side. Claydon took one step back and shot the third with his pistol. The second had evaded the tomahawk. He had a bad gash on the shoulder but he was advancing on Harpe, so Claydon got behind him and used the knife again.

Harpe looked down at the bloody deck, at the five corpses. "It always ends so soon," he said.

Claydon answered, "The sooner, the better," and wiped his knife on the tail of his hunting shirt.

Harpe was recovering his gold from the old man's clenched hand. The man groaned and moved, and Harpe used the tomahawk. Then he ripped off the old man's shirt and found a rawhide wallet heavy with gold.

Claydon's eyes glittered when he saw the weight of the wallet. "We'd better get off the boat before another comes around the bend."

Harpe scowled as he dropped the tomahawk back in its loop. "We can't leave the boat like this. They'd get posses out to look for us. And what about Sam Mason?"

"He wouldn't know who did it."

"He'd know when he saw their heads split open."

"We can dump 'em in the river."

"No." Harpe was positive. "Take the bodies below, and fasten them so they won't come afloat."

Claydon stared at him, then upriver. He put the knife back in his shirt and picked up two men by the collars and dragged them across the deck to the opening. He dumped them below and turned back. Harpe was behind him with two more. "Get down there," he said. "Use some rope to tie them so the bodies won't come up."

Claydon jumped down. He found a coil of rope and tied the five bodies close together, each by a leg, and tied the rope to the center scaffolding that held up the deck. When he got back on top he was breathless. "The boat is filled with skins," he said. "Fox, wolf, bear, beaver, mink—this cargo is worth thousands of dollars in Natchez!"

Harpe was unimpressed. "Not to us," he said. "Let's sink her." They went below, and Harpe led him to the side away from the shore and began to knock out the chinking with his tomahawk. Within ten minutes the water was pouring through the cracks, and the boat began to settle on that side. "So she won't founder in the mud," said Harpe.

They went back up. Still there was no other boat in the visible stretch of the river. Harpe took the old man's wallet out of his shirt. He gave Claydon half a dozen coins, took half a dozen himself, and then threw the wallet and its remaining contents out into the river.

Claydon gulped. "That's good money!"

"You're a fool!" Harpe growled. "If we have too much, Mason will find it out." He went to one knee and cut the mooring rope with the tomahawk. It parted suddenly, the long end snapping back. The boat seemed to hesitate a moment until the force of the current took hold. Then, listing toward the center of the river, and pushed by the breeze, she began to float away. Harpe glanced upriver. "Nobody in sight. We're safe." He jumped overboard with a splash, and Claydon followed.

"She'll float toward the center and sink," Harpe said, "and it'll be years before anybody will even be sure she's gone—and maybe never. Hundreds of boats comin' down. Nobody knows if they don't get to New

Orleans."

"But that money—"

"Money!" Harpe growled. "You got enough money to buy all the wimmen in the Gallo Negro at Natchez for a week."

"I git tired of them kind," said Claydon. "I'd like to make enough money to go up on the hill sometime."

"You better stay off the hill. I hear they're going to have a sheriff up there." He stared at Claydon.

Claydon felt the sweat coming out on his pale forehead, and kept his tongue with an effort. He was a big man, and quick and strong, and he knew it. He didn't kill for the same reason as Harpe, but those he killed were just as dead when he finished. No, he had no fear of Harpe, though he did resent his tongue sometimes. The main thing was that Harpe had Sam Mason's confidence and that he didn't care about money. That was ideal for Claydon. He had now seven caches along the Trace, and one of them was a handful of jewelry with real diamonds. He could afford to be patient, for Harpe was helping him. Harpe took the orders. Harpe explained to Mason when they found no gold. And Mason believed him. Claydon took a deep, satisfied breath. He could not complain.

CHAPTER IX

ZER FOLEY STARED AT NATHAN AND THEN AT THE bullet hole in Pete Brandon's back. He looked at the south ridge, at the north ridge, at the cabin. That shot could have come from anywhere. Pete had been turning when he was hit. Zer's lips tightened into white lines. "There'll be hell to pay for this day's work," he said.

More shots came from the cabin. Zer looked that way, then toward the south ridge. A man was making his way down from the ridge on a horse. Zer ran to the cabin.

"Quit shooting, you fools!" he cried. "You've done enough already!"

"That's Bill Brandon's roan," said Tim.

Zer waited above the dead boy. He waited until Bill Brandon broke into the open meadow, and then stepped back.

Brandon reached the body and slid off the roan, his mouth tight. He went to his son's side and knelt in the dust. He listened for the heartbeat and tried the pulse. Finally he got up and stood for a moment with his head bowed.

More men were now coming across the meadow, and others were descending from the steep north ridge in single file.

Brandon's face was stark. He said in a choked voice to Zer, "He's dead."

Zer said, "God, I'm sorry, Bill."

Brandon stood there and looked down at the bare back with the red welt and the small black hole just under the heart. "Somebody's goin' to pay for this," he said harshly. "Not even a Foley can murder my son for shootin' a deer."

Zer said cautiously, "We don't know whose shot killed him."

"No—but we know almighty well if that crazy Mat hadn't tried to whip him, this wouldn't have happened. Who in hell does Mat Foley think he is—God almighty—that he can go around whipping people whenever he damn' pleases?"

Zer said nothing, but kept his eyes on the ground.

The men from the south ridge, led by black-mustached Fred Evans, came around the black willow tree. There were seven of them.

Nine men from the north ridge splashed across the creek, led by the whiskered Jim Sigler, carrying a long rifle, and brought up in the rear by Elisha Wilson, who seemed about half drunk. They all gathered around Pete's body, and Evans got down. "So they killed him," he said, and there was real bitterness in his voice. He raised his head and looked at the cabin. "Mat Foley finally had his way—all the way!"

"Wait a minute," said Zer. "This is no way to settle this."

Evans looked up at Zer, who was the spitting image of what Mat Foley had been twenty years before. "You can say that! It isn't your kid lying on the ground with the buzzards circling over!"

Jim Sigler said coldly, "I've scalped many an Indian fer less than that." He looked toward the cabin. "It don't look to me like Mat Foley is any better than an Indian."

"You still don't know where the shot came from," said Zer.

"It doesn't make any difference," said Evans. "He's dead."

Bill Brandon was staring toward the cabin with a

peculiar glassiness in his eyes. "We can take 'em!" he said.

Elisha Wilson said, "There cain't be over three or four of 'em in there."

"What are you talking about?" demanded Evans.

"They killed my kid," said Brandon.

"When I come into Kentucky," said Jim Sigler, "we took care of things like this."

"Kentucky isn't like it was," said Evans. "There's law here now."

"What good is law," demanded Brandon, "when a feller like him can whip and kill your kid?"

Nathan saw Fred Evans, black-haired and stocky, staring somberly at the corpse of Pete Brandon.

Evans said: "You don't need an answer to that. You know how hard we fought to get law into this county. Now we've got a sheriff and a judge, and I say let them do the work they're supposed to do."

"What if they turn the damn' coyote loose?" asked Brandon.

"We'll face that when it comes. Now, men, let's get back to the Crossroads. I'm going to find Sidney Morse and make a complaint. Then the sheriff can come out here and arrest him legal."

Brandon looked at the body still on the ground.

Zer said quietly, "I'll get you a wagon, Bill, and a team." Brandon looked at him. "You've always been a pretty good feller," he said, and shook his head. "But you're too much like Mat. You'll start playin' God some day, and you'll git struck by lightnin'."

Zer motioned Nathan and Tim to come with him. They went behind the storeroom and rolled out a light wagon. Nathan and Tim went across the creek and caught up two work horses, harnessed them to the wagon, and drove it to the straw pile, where Zer forked the bed full of straw. Then Nathan drove the team slowly up to the group of silent men. He wrapped the reins around the whip socket and got down. "I'm sorry, Mr. Brandon. Terrible sorry."

Bill Brandon's mouth was white around his lips. Without answering, he just looked at Nathan and then bent down to the body of his boy. Fred Evans helped him pick Pete up and lay him in the straw. Fred said: "Tie your horse to the end-gate. I'll drive."

They got in the spring seat together. "Leave the wagon at the livery," said Nathan. "We'll call for it later."

Brandon nodded. "I'll leave it," he said. "But you ain't heerd the last of this—not by a damn' sight."

Nathan was sure of it. He was glad to see the cortege line out on the road to town. He looked at Tim, who had come up beside him. Tim's face was wet with sweat.

"We're lucky," he said. "Lucky they didn't start up the valley, killin' and burnin'."

Nathan looked at the wagon, going very slowly, and at the long line of riders following it. All of them carried rifles. He looked back at Tim. "It isn't too late yet."

Zer was coming around the corner of the cabin. "We were lucky," he said, "mighty lucky." He shook his head. "They could of wiped out the whole valley."

He pushed open the door, and they all went in. Mat was sitting at the table with a cup of rye. George McGee was still at the narrow oiled-skin window, with his rifle poked through one corner, and Nathan noted that his rifle covered the spot where Pete had been killed. From that moment Nathan loathed George McGee, for he knew instinctively it was McGee who had shot the boy. None of the men on the ridges would have taken a

89

chance on a shot close enough to hit Pete. Nathan looked around the cabin and saw that, unless somebody had been shooting from the open door, which wasn't likely, the shot must have come from McGee's window.

Zer sat down heavily, opposite his father. "You played hell this time," he said.

Mat's deep eyes were burning. His shoulder wound hadn't been dressed yet. "When I catch somebody on my land, I got a right to run them off."

"Sure you have," said Zer, pouring a cup of whisky, "but you've got no right to punish them—certainly no right to whip anybody. That can be done only by the law."

"In this valley," Mat Foley said stubbornly, "I *am* the law."

"You'll be lucky to stay in this valley another thirty days," said Zer.

George McGee pulled his rifle out of the window opening and turned around. "What's to get so het up about?"

"If it was your kid," said Zer, "you'd be het up too." He studied McGee. "Or wouldn't you?"

"What do you mean by that?"

Zer sneered at him. "Don't threaten me or I'll break you in two. You know damn' well what I mean: the only thing you care about is how much you're getting out of it."

McGee was livid. "I ought to shoot you down for sayin' that!"

"If you did," Zer said contemptuously, "you'd find me better sport than a kid with a pack of bear dogs tearing him to pieces." McGee brought up the rifle, but Nathan grasped the long barrel with both hands and tore it away from him. He walked to the door and threw the rifle as far as he could with one hand. He went back in and said to McGee, "You *must* be touched in the head." Zer emptied the cup and refilled it. "Boys playin' at a man's game," he said, "are likely to git hurt." He looked at McGee. "It *was* you," he said. "You're a maniac behind a rifle."

Mat asked heavily, "Did you kill him, George?"

"I was shootin' at the dogs," said George.

Nathan was contemptuous. "You shot the kid," he said, "because you thought nobody would know who did it. That's the way you do everything."

McGee turned to look at him with surprise, and it struck Nathan that he *should* have been surprised, for Nathan, ten years younger, had taken his rifle away from him and had rebuked him.

Joe, the fat Foley, got up. "I guess I'll go home," he said.

Zer looked at him. "You'd better pack," he told him.

"What do you mean?" asked Bert. "Nobody can prove anything."

"You don't think an old Injun fighter like Bill Brandon is goin' to take this layin' down, do you?"

"I don't know what he can do."

"You'll damn' soon find out. You want somebody takin' a potshot at you every time you set foot outside your place?"

"We can shoot back," said McGee, getting up.

"Sure," said Zer. "Only this time you're shootin' at a grown man hidin' in the forest."

"In the forest." McGee was trying to recover his courage. "Sure, they drop like squirrels when you hit 'em."

"And they shoot back like Indians—but a lot straighter."

91

Joe went out to the horse pen, and a few minutes later he loped across the grass toward his place.

Nathan opened the door and looked down the road. The wagon was out of sight, and the leading horseman was just coming up out of a dip. Nathan went back and sat down at the table. He took the demijohn on his right arm and poured a drink.

Bert looked at Zer and then at Mat. "What do we do now?" he asked.

"It ain't our move," said Zer.

Pounding hoofs were approaching the cabin, and Nathan opened the door to look out. Nancy McGee, riding sidesaddle, her hair confined in a calico sundown, was pulling up to the cabin. She turned the horse over to Abraham and got down.

Nathan held the door open for her, but she didn't look at him. She swept into the middle of the room, her eyes seeking George. "What kind of trouble have you gone and got yourself mixed up in now?" she demanded.

George had stopped reloading his rifle. "Now, Nancy, I—"

"Isn't there enough trouble, without getting the town people down on us?"

"We aren't in any trouble, Nancy," George pleaded.

"You're always in trouble. You don't know enough to wipe your nose. You—" Nancy went on and on, and no one did or said anything. Actually there was nothing to do or say. Nathan watched her, thinking that her nose was as sharp as her tongue, and wondering what it was that had made her such an unhappy woman—for surely no happy woman would talk the way she did.

"You'd be better off taking the dogs and looking for a bear. We've got to have oil for the winter—unless you want to use your own hogs."

"It's only the last of September, Nancy," George whined. "There's plenty of time yet. The bears won't hibernate for two, three months."

It was easy enough to see what was the matter with George; it wasn't so easy to understand Nancy. She'd had everything she wanted; her father had always pampered her.

Nathan thought to look at Mat. Though Mat was sitting straight and square as usual, his left arm was lying on the table, oddly limp, and Nathan saw that a little pool of blood was collecting under Mat's elbow. But Mat gave no sign of pain. He sat with his eyes slightly narrowed as he watched and listened to Nancy, and it was hard to tell what he was thinking, though his eyes smoldered under his shock of grizzled red hair.

"I told you before," Nancy was telling George in her shrill voice, "to stay out of trouble with the town people. Now you've gone and got in bad with them. What have you done, anyway? Why were they down here? What did they take a wagon back for?"

George squirmed, with his sharp little black eyes watching Nancy and darting around to the others, but always coming back to Nancy. But George didn't open his mouth, and Nancy wouldn't close hers.

"I've told you and told you and told you to stay up there on your farm and mind your own business, and now you come down here and get mixed up in something that's none of your affair. Why don't you do what you're told?"

Nathan would slap her face if she ever talked that way to him—but not George. He was too concerned with his stake in the Foley estate; that was always uppermost in his mind. That was why, Nathan knew, he had shot Pete Brandon: he had wanted to make an

93

impression on Mat. And now he sat there like a treed coon and didn't even show his teeth. Nathan was disgusted.

"There's fence to mend, and hogs to slop, and cows to milk. Why aren't you up there doing your chores?"

Zer turned up his tin cup and looked at Nancy. "You talk too much," he said, and in that moment he was the spitting image of Mat Foley in looks and voice and movement. He was Mat Foley with the sense that Mat must have had when he was younger. Nathan wondered if Zer would start playing God when he got older— maybe when Mat died.

Nancy didn't look at Zer. She had better sense than to tangle with her older brother. She kept berating George.

"What of me, staying up there in that cabin by myself and hearing rifles go off down here? Do you think I was happy? Do you think I could sit down and spin yarn while you was down here in a battle with the town people? Don't you have any feeling for me at all?"

Mat's glance flicked across George's face with contempt. Then he filled his cup without moving his left arm. There was a considerable pool of blood on the table now.

"Ma," he said, without turning his head, "you better dress my shoulder." He took a drink. "And bring your knittin' needles. The bullet's still in there." He finished the cup of rye. "Some damn' tightwad was usin' a short charge of gunpowder."

94

CHAPTER X

NATHAN RODE INTO TOWN THE NEXT DAY TO GET THE wagon. Jason Carr, the one-armed liveryman, had little to say until Nathan prodded him. "Well, it were a sad thing," he admitted. "Pete was the only kin Bill Brandon had. Bill is takin' it hard, I hear."

"Threats?"

"In a way. Nothin' personal. Judge Endicott will be back from Danville tonight, and he'll call a grand jury, no doubt."

"Trouble is," said Nathan, "nobody knows who fired the shot—do they?"

"Not as far as I heerd, but somebody sure did—and it wouldn't of happened if Pete hadn't been getting whipped. The people around here figure it's on Mat's shoulders."

"Seems to me it's a legal question," said Nathan.

Jason finished hooking the traces and took off his old hat, wiping his forehead with a dirty, colored handkerchief held in the same hand. "You've changed since you moved into Foley's valley," he said. "I don't know how you stand on this, and I ain't askin', but I'll tell you something: there's people here who say that if Mat Foley is beyond the law, he sure as hell isn't beyond the reach of public opinion."

"What do they figure on doing about it?"

"It ain't rightly up to me to say."

He paid Jason and watched the man put the money in his clasp purse; it was astonishing what a man could do with one hand. He drove the team to Farnum's Tavern, tied it to the hitch rail, and walked inside.

95

Half a dozen men were drinking at the tables, and five were playing monte on an upended cracker barrel. They were all rough men, roughly dressed. Some wore powder horns, and most wore knives or tomahawks. The habits of the frontier had not worn off yet.

A man facing the door, with a cup of whisky at his mouth, froze when Nathan walked in, the tin cup suspended. The others saw the cessation of movement, and turned about with one motion to stare at Nathan. The monte game stopped for a moment, and the five men looked his way. Nathan looked at them all, without hostility but with a certain amount of trepidation. Then he walked across to the counter where old Mr. Fairfax looked at him over his square glasses. "Something?"

"Five pounds of salt," said Nathan.

Mr. Fairfax pulled the cover off of a small keg. "Just got in some fresh from the Falls."

Nathan said nothing. He was conscious of the eyes fixed on him, the lack of movement in the room. He waited for Mr. Fairfax to sack it up and weigh it on his old scale. "That'll be one dollar even."

Nathan slid a Spanish peso across the counter. He picked up the sack and went to the door. All eyes followed him, as if they belonged to one head. He got to the door and remembered something. He wheeled suddenly and faced their stares for an instant. Then he went back to the counter. "Got any coffee?"

"Sure, plenty. Shipment came up the river from New Orleans the other day." He pulled a board from the head of a hogshead and began to shovel out the whole beans with a scoop. "How much you figure?"

"Five pounds."

"Have to have eighty cents a pound for this here. Costs money to ship it in, you know."

Mr. Fairfax's voice was high and reedy; too high, Nathan thought. He watched him tie a string around the sack. "When is Pete's funeral?" he asked in a low voice.

"Tomorrow." Mr. Fairfax looked at him over his glasses. "But I wouldn't go, if I was you."

"Somebody's got to go."

"Somebody may get hurt before it's over."

"I don't want trouble," said Nathan. "I'll come unarmed." Mr. Fairfax took the money. "Be better if you didn't."

"It wouldn't look good if we all stayed away. We aren't all of us trying to start a feud."

"You've got nothin' to gain by comin'."

"I'm not trying to gain anything. I'm coming to show my respect for Pete Brandon."

"It's pretty late for that."

"Not as far as I'm concerned. I never had a rifle and I never fired a shot. I never backed up anybody who did, and I wasn't there when the whipping started. Zer and Tim and I were riding down to stop it."

"Pity you didn't get there sooner."

"I believe that," said Nathan.

"Only thing is," said Mr. Fairfax, "you married Sarah, and that makes you a Foley."

"I don't feel that way."

"The way you feel has got nothin' to do with it," said Mr. Fairfax. "It's the way the people feel."

Nathan took a package under each arm and started out. A whiskered man stood up suddenly and barred his way to the door. "So you ain't no red Foley, eh?"

"No."

"You sleep in a Foley bed, don't you?"

Nathan hesitated. "I sleep in my own bed." But his voice lacked sureness, for it wasn't exactly true. He

97

hadn't made the cabin with his own hands, and he hadn't bought the land with his own money. The property was all Mat's.

The man sneered. "So you ain't no Foley, eh? I say you are—and I say this country is damn' well glutted with Foleys."

Nathan looked at him, saw the glittering belligerence in his eyes, and knew what was coming. "You've got your mind made up," he said. "What are you going to do about it?"

The man moved closer. "Starting right now," he said, "I'm goin' to make one of 'em wish he was somewhere else besides up in that valley where they breed like pigs."

Nathan shoved the bag of salt at the whiskered face. It broke as the man got his hands on Nathan's throat. The salt filled the man's eyes and left him blinded. Nathan stood in the middle of the room. "Anybody else?" he asked.

A huge backwoodsman stood up. "I say you can't get rid of me with a sack full of salt," he drawled, and launched himself at Nathan across the table.

Nathan dropped the bag of coffee and leaped to meet him. They closed and rolled on the table. They went to the floor, and Nathan could feel the coffee beans under his back. The backwoodsman flailed at his face with his dirty nails. Nathan dodged and leaped up. The man got his thumb under Nathan's jaw and began to work his middle finger into the corner of Nathan's eyes. Nathan choked him until he felt the cartilage give in the man's Adam's apple, but the long finger worked under his eyeball and popped it out on his cheek. Nathan reared back, got the man's wrist in his grip, and brought it down on the edge of the table. He heard the bone crack,

98

but he was furious with pain. He picked up an empty keg and hurled it into the man's face, then followed it with fists, elbows, and knees. The man doubled over, his hands at his groin. Nathan gave him one last battering with his doubled fists, and the man went down.

Nathan stood breathing harshly for a moment before he reached up to the eye that was lying on his cheek. With one hand he separated the eyelids and with the other he pressed the eyeball back into place. He was temporarily blind in one eye.

There was silence in the room for a moment. Then Mr. Fairfax said in his high, reedy voice, "I'll scoop up some more salt for you."

Nathan gathered himself and took a deep breath. Though his eye hurt like fire, and he felt that it would ache for weeks, he walked unsteadily back to the counter. "I still need coffee too," he said, and waited while Mr. Fairfax sacked it up. Then he took one sack under each arm, as before, and started for the door. The big man with the broken arm, and probably with a broken voice box too, was sitting slumped in a corner while someone tried to pour whisky into his mouth from a tin cup.

"Somebody'd better get him a doctor," said Nathan, and walked out.

He drove to the valley, left the wagon behind the storeroom at Mat's place, unhitched the team, and drove them across the creek.

Mat came out as he was mounting the gelding. "You got the team all right?"

"Sure," said Nathan.

Mat's left arm was hanging limp. "Looks like you been in a fight."

"Yeah," said Nathan, and rode off.

At home, Sarah met him outside. "There's blood on your face," she said, "and your eye—it's—Nate, you've had a fight!"

"Have you got any hot water inside?" he asked. "I want some packs on my left eye."

White and shaken, she hastened into the house to get the compresses ready.

Though Nathan's pain eased somewhat with the hot packs, he slept little that night, and along toward morning he said, "We've got to go to the funeral today."

"Do you think we should?"

"Yes," he said firmly. "There'll be trouble."

"There's already been trouble."

She looked at his set face. "All right, Nathan, whatever you say." They drove to town in the buggy and stood by the open grave while the homemade coffin, fitted with store-bought casket handles, was lowered into the grave with bridle reins.

Bill Brandon stood at the foot end of the grave. He had been well plied with liquor. The Reverend Waters stood at the other end with a Bible in his hands. Sarah was weeping softly, and Nathan noticed that they had been left to stand alone on one side of the grave, while the remaining mourners crowded together on the opposite side.

Though it was a cool day, the sun shone warm on their bare heads. After the preacher had spoken words of comfort and admonished the father and the rest of his hearers to bear no malice toward any man, for "inscrutable is God in His great wisdom," Elisha Wilson and Jim Sigler began to fill the grave. Then the Reverend Waters repeated, "Ashes to ashes and dust to dust." Bill Brandon looked on dry-eyed, but his thoughts seemed far away. Perhaps he was thinking of Pete's mother, and of the day Pete was born.

As the small crowd drifted away, Nathan left with his head down, his arm around Sarah's waist. His left eye ached badly, and the little vision he had through it was blurred.

It was late afternoon when they pulled up at the stream near Mat's place. Mat came out and asked briefly, "They get him buried?"

"Yes."

Mat nodded. Maybe he felt some sympathy for the kid, Nathan thought, but he had lost none of his old arrogance. "Too bad," Mat said.

Nathan drove on up the valley. Tim walked out from his cornfield to meet them. "Any trouble?" he asked.

Nathan looked down at him as he pulled up the horse. "No."

"Your eye looks funny."

"Hurt it yesterday."

"Oh."

Bert Foley was watching them from a seat under a chestnut tree. Zer was in the field; he paused to look up, but did not come to meet them. Ben Metheny stayed inside—if he was inside. They continued up the valley.

"George is coming to meet us," said Sarah, pulling her shawl closer about her.

George crossed the creek on a coon bridge. "You go to the funeral?" His black eyes were probing.

"Yes," said Nathan.

"Trouble?"

"Did you expect some?"

George swallowed. "Not necessarily."

"You weren't in a place where you could have any trouble—this time."

George blustered. "What you talkin' about?"

"You," said Nathan.

George came to the side of the buggy. "Why are you layin' it into me?"

Nathan stared at him coldly.

"You figger I should—" George said.

"I figger you should keep your mouth shut unless you've got something to say."

George went on the defensive. "You married a Foley too, didn't you?"

"I sure did," answered Nathan, "but it hasn't made a coward of me." He snapped the buggy whip. "Git up!" he said.

CHAPTER XI

NOTHING HAPPENED UNTIL THE THIRD DAY. ON THAT morning Nathan got up late. He had dozed off about midnight, after the hot packs, and had got his first good night's sleep. He was beginning to see out of the eye too, and he felt considerably better as he drank his morning coffee. He was putting away a big slice of fried pork and ashcake when Henry, their black man, came to the door.

"They's trouble down at the big house, sub."

Nathan looked up. "What kind of trouble?"

"I don' know, suh. People gath'rin' down theah."

"I'll be out," said Nathan.

"You want I should saddle the geldin', suh?"

"Yes. "

Sarah looked frightened. "What do you think it is now?"

"I don't know."

"Something about Mother?"

He shook his head and drained his coffee cup.

He loped the gelding down the valley. Bert and Joe Foley were there; he saw their horses. Tim Hagans joined him as he rode. "Know what it is?" asked Nathan.

"No. I was piling hickory in the smokehouse when Alice called me."

Mat was walking up and down in front of the cabin, swinging his lame arm and swearing a blue streak. The yard was littered with dog carcasses—five of them, already beginning to bloat. Nathan got down.

Mat's face was filled with fury. "Somebody threw out

103

poisoned meat to my dogs last night!"

Nathan looked around. "All of them?"

"Every last one."

Nathan looked at him coolly. "It might have been worse," he said. "It might have been children."

Mat swore again.

"Do you know when it happened?"

"Along towards morning," Mat said, "the dogs set up a fuss. It didn't last long, and I figured it was an owl or something. But about sunup Abraham came to the door and said the dogs was dead."

"Somebody must have ridden up with a tow sack full of raw meat loaded with strychnine," Nathan said. "When the dogs began to bark, they threw out the meat, then turned around and went back. Strychnine works fast on dogs," he observed.

"If I had two good arms I'd—"

"You'd what?"

"I'd ride into the Crossroads and nail Bill Brandon to the side of the livery stable."

"In the first place," Nathan observed, "the people wouldn't let you. The Foleys aren't popular up there right now. And in the second place, you don't know who did this."

"I can't prove it," said Mat, "but I know damn' well who did it."

"Somebody might say the same about the shooting of Bill Brandon's kid," said Nathan.

"Who the hell's side are you on?" Mat demanded.

"I'm trying to show you you're headed for trouble. Judge Endicott called a grand jury for yesterday to investigate Pete Brandon's killing. The best thing any of us can do is stay away from the Crossroads and stay out of Farnum's Tavern."

"There's no place in Kentucky I'm a-feared to go," said Mat.

"Then you better start getting scared right now. The Crossroads is no place for any of us until the people cool off."

"Where am I goin' to get supplies?"

"Send Ben Metheny up to the Falls. *He* likes to keep out of trouble."

Bert tied a rope around a dog's leg, got on his horse, and dragged the bloated carcass down the road and off to one side. He came back dragging the rope.

"It'll stink like hell if the wind blows up the creek," said Mat.

Bert pointed to two buzzards already started on their slow spirals high above the tops of the ridges. "There won't be anything left by afternoon," he said. He fastened the rope around the leg of a second dog and loped off.

Mat said, "Come on in."

Mat's wife was in a corner sewing blocks together for a red-white-and-blue Goose Eye quilt. She didn't look up. Mat poured whisky with his good arm. "Help yourselves," he said. "We've got to hold a council of war."

"There's nothing to hold a council about," Nathan said. "There's nothing we can do unless we catch somebody—and I don't think we're going to do that."

"Nate's right," said Zer, coming in the door. "There's not a damn' thing we can do but sweat it out."

"I never been one to sit still and let the other feller take a potshot at me," said Mat.

"This time is different," Zer told him. "The country's been changing. This ain't Indian country no more. Things have to be done legal."

"Is it legal to poison a man's dogs?"

"No more than it's legal to shoot a man's son in the back," said Zer.

"A lot of talk," said Mat. "An almighty lot of talk, but nobody's doing anything—and I've only got one good arm."

Zer sat down and helped himself to the whisky. "It wouldn't make any difference if you had ten good arms. You started something that's going to be hard to stop."

"What do we do in the meantime?"

"Like I said—wait."

Nathan had never seen Mat look baffled before, but he was seeing it now. Joe Foley slouched in and helped himself to a cup.

"It's my valley," Mat said stubbornly. "I won this valley by myself."

Zer shook his head. "No, you didn't. In the first place, no one man whipped the Indians out of Kentucky. In the second place, you had no organized opposition when you came into this valley. You bought out the settlers one at a time, and they allowed you to because they weren't set on staying here anyway. But now you've got something bigger, Mat. You've got the whole country against you." He shook his head again. "Besides, you're the one who is tryin' to stay put, so you're the one to get shot at."

"We could throw guards up on the ridges."

"It wouldn't do any good. They'd never find anybody."

That night someone got in Bert Foley's chicken house and cut the throats of nearly a hundred pullets.

The next night Tim's smokehouse burned, with eighteen hams and several hundred pounds of bacon.

Ben Metheny went up to the Falls for a load of flour.

On the way back, a rear wheel broke when he was fording the creek, and most of the flour was spoiled. It might have been saved, but Ben, as usual, was drunk. Zer found two of the spokes on the broken wheel whittled down to the size of a man's little finger.

Two nights after that, the big boulder that overhung Nathan's place came down in the middle of a cold, driving rain. It crashed through the roof of the harness shed and made kindling wood out of the buggy. A six-inch log had been used to pry the rock loose.

That day Nathan went into town. He turned the gelding in at the livery stable and asked Jason Carr, "What happened to that grand jury?"

Carr fastened the gate with his one arm. "They recessed. Since they didn't know who shot the boy, there waren't much they could do."

Nathan went to the tavern. Three men were sitting at a table, but when Nathan came in they got up one at a time and walked out. Mr. Fairfax whittled a sliver of tobacco and popped it into his mouth.

"I'll need a sack of sugar," Nathan said.

Fairfax looked at him steadily. "Happens I'm out of sugar, Nate."

"Well, give me a couple bundles of cigars."

"Cigars ain't come in from Virginia yet. Waitin' on the new crop, I reckon."

Nathan frowned. "How about coffee?"

"Coffee's a little short too."

Nathan stared at him. Fairfax hadn't moved. "You turnin' me down?"

"I told you—I'm out."

Nathan's anger began to rise. "You've never been out of that many things since I've known you."

The old man leaned over the counter and spoke in a

husky whisper. "You don't want to get in trouble, do you, Nate?"

"I'm in trouble already. I need supplies."

"If *you* don't mind gettin' in more trouble—how about me?"

"You?"

"The talk is," said Fairfax, "that anybody in this part of the country who sells supplies for the State of Foley might wake up some night with his store burned down."

Nathan looked at him a long time. "All right," he said finally, and turned on his heel.

Nathan followed the ridge road on the way back. He dropped down out of the woods and followed the trail past Zer's place. The dogs came barking to meet him, and Zer straightened up from where he was fixing a piece of fence. "They won't let us buy supplies at the Crossroads," Nathan said.

Zer swore.

"It looks like we'll have to get together and take a wagon to the Falls. "

Zer laid his ax against a big rock. "If enough of us went to the Crossroads together—" The ax handle jerked and fell to the ground, splintered. A bullet whined down toward the creek, and the report of a rifle came from the forest above them.

Zer jumped up and glared at the small puff of black powder smoke drifting toward the tree tops. He scowled. "If they want a war," he growled, "they'll get one."

The rock seemed to explode, and slivers shot out and stung the backs of Nathan's hands. Again came the report of a rifle.

Zer shook his fist at the spot in the woods and swore long and vehemently. Then he turned abruptly to

Nathan. "Have you got the guts to go to the Falls with me for supplies tomorrow?"

"I'll do it."

"We better be out of the valley before it gets light."

Nathan nodded and moved off. He rode up the valley slowly, and Sarah met him at the door. "I heard rifle shots," she said. Nathan got down slowly. "You'll hear more."

He put the gelding in the pen and went to the cabin. Sarah was roasting a ham in the fireplace. Nathan took his rifle down from the deer horns. He took it to the fireplace and discharged it up the chimney, then came back and laid it on the homemade table. He got the powder gourd from under the bed and the bullet pouch from a peg on the wall. Sarah watched him in worried silence. He put a lead ball in the palm of his cupped hand and covered it with powder. He picked out the ball and laid it on the table, held the long rifle's butt on the floor, and poured the powder down the muzzle, using his hand as a funnel. He took a small square patch of cloth from the bullet pouch and laid it over the muzzle, then placed the ball in the center. He pulled out the long ramrod, put the concave end over the bullet, and pushed it down with one clean stroke. He examined the flint, glanced at the firing pan, and then set the rifle back on the deer horns.

As he cleared away the bullet pouch and powder gourd, Sarah asked with a certain quiet fatalism that he had learned to recognize in her voice, "Nate, is there going to be more trouble?"

Nathan looked down at her and put one big hand on her shoulder, his fingers spread a little to feel her vitality through the rough cloth of her homespun dress. Sarah never had faced anything like this before. He said carefully, "Zer and I are going to the Falls in the morning."

He felt her grow taut under his fingers. She took a deep breath, and then another. Finally the tautness relaxed a little. She looked up at him. Her eyes were haunted. "Nate, I don't know how I can raise a baby without you—" She drew another breath. Her eyes did not leave his. "But do what you think best."

It was a great relief. His big fingers tightened on her shoulder. "Thanks, Sarah," he said softly. "I figure on being around when your time comes."

He had trouble getting to sleep. A couple of times he got up and prowled the cabin, opening the door softly and searching the edge of the forest down the valley, for the moon was high and every detail in the valley was plain in the frosty air. But each time he found nothing.

Sarah was awake too, and each time he came back she moved against him silently. He went to sleep around midnight, and it seemed he had hardly dozed off before he woke again. He looked at the stars and said, "Time to go."

Sarah was there, like a wraith in her nightdress, for the moon had gone down and the valley was in dense darkness. "Be careful, Nate."

He nodded, touched her shoulders again, got his rifle, powderhorn, and bullet pouch, took the small package of dried meat and journeycake, and stepped out into the darkness.

For a moment he stood there, listening. The valley itself was quiet except for Zer's place, from which came subdued clinking as Zer harnessed the team. Up on the mountain behind Nathan's place a wolf howled and an owl hooted, but across the valley there was no sound, and Nathan paused. Along the ridge toward Zer's place too, he noticed, there was no sound. He gripped his rifle and stepped off into the darkness. He heard the cabin door close softly behind him. Then he was swinging down the trail diagonally across the meadow. He hit Zer's cornfield at one end. The stubble was dry and crisp, but he walked down the rows and avoided stepping on the stalks.

At Zer's barn he stepped around the corner and said in a low voice, "It's me, Zer."

An answer came: "Put your rifle by the seat and give me a hand with the team." He went on, grumbling, "I figured to use the biggest four-horse team I had, to save time, but that bay wheel horse is snortin' this time of morning, and I got the damn' breeching turned inside out."

Nathan put his rifle in the wagon. "Have you noticed how quiet it is?"

"Yeah. I s'pose they're watchin' us."

Nathan unhooked the near side strap and untwisted the breeching, poked the strap through a couple of times, then felt along the harness to see that it was straight. Zer was hooking the breast straps into the ring at the end of the pole. The bay took a sudden kick at Nathan, but he had his hand on her haunches for the purpose of feeling her movements, and stepped back quickly. The bay's hoof thudded against the singletree.

"Damn!" said Zer. "I forgot to tell you that horse likes to kick so early in the morning."

"No harm," said Nathan. "I wouldn't trust any horse this time of day."

They got into the wagon seat. Nathan released the brake, and Zer wheeled the big four-horse team and followed the trail to the creek. He kept the team at a walk, but there was the muffled thud of hoofs on dirt,

111

clinking of trace chains, creak of leather, the rumble of the wide-tired wagon, and the slow creak of boards as they rubbed against one another when one wheel dropped into a hole or went over a hump.

They turned opposite Ben Metheny's place. It was quiet. "Fine dogs he's got," Zer said in a low voice. "As lazy as Ben himself."

Tim's place was away from the road, and they rumbled on down the creek, the wagon beginning now to make hollow sounds as the horses picked up their pace. Zer braced his feet against the bed and hauled back on the reins to keep them from going into a trot.

There were no dogs at Mat's place, but a low hail came from the door of the big cabin. "Who's drivin'?"

"Zer."

"Wait up a minute."

Zer pulled the team to a stop. Mat came out to the wagon. "Who's with you?"

"Nate. "

"Goin' to the Falls?"

"Yes. "

"Old man Fairfax won't let you have anything at the store?"

"The people won't allow him to," said Nathan.

He could almost feel Mat swell up below him. "The whole country is turned against us?"

"Just about."

"Then to hell with 'em. We'll pick up and go to the Tejas Country."

That was always Mat's way: no middle path. All or nothing—and all his way.

Zer loosened the reins. "In the meantime," he said, "we've got to have supplies."

They rattled along at a good clip. The forest came

112

down to the road on the right, and between the road and the creek on the left was about twenty feet of brush—wild plums, leatherwood, and cucumber vines.

They rode in silence, Zer holding back against the team with the four reins coming in under his hands, the loose ends hanging down over his thumbs. He said presently, "I figger—"

A flash of red and yellow fire came from the trees in the face of the lead off horse. The horse reared. Zer jerked hard on the reins. A flash came from the brush opposite, and both horses reared. Zer began to swear as he manhandled the reins to keep the team in the road. But more flashes began to pour from both sides, and the valley—almost a canyon down here—reverberated with the crash and roll of rifle fire.

"Damn! Damn! Damn!" shouted Zer.

The lead horses pulled to the right but were met with more fire. The team swung toward the creek. The smell of gunpowder was strong. The tail end of the wagon crashed against a poplar tree, and the corner of the wagon dropped as the wheel gave way with a screech of riving hickory spokes. More flashes from the right, with the crash of explosions in the horses' ears. The team plunged into the brush, and there was nothing Zer could do but try to hold them back. But they were galloping, and Zer might as well not have had the reins. The wagon bounced over the rough brush. There was one last rifle shot, and by it Nathan saw the face of Bill Brandon. Hanging onto the bucking wagon, he shot a glance at Zer. But Zer had his hands full. Nathan looked back to the front.

He heard the splash as the team charged into the creek, and he was drenched with cold water. Then the wagon dropped two feet. The team turned upstream, back toward the valley. The left rear wheel collapsed against a boulder, and the entire back end of the wagon went down. The team was fighting now, frantic. They reared and plunged, each one trying to get loose from the wagon. Within fifty feet a front wheel dropped into a hole, the wagon spun halfway, then the team lunged once more, and the wagon went over.

Zer and Nathan were thrown clear. Nathan went into the water and came up spluttering. The team was still dragging the wagon. Nathan ran after them.

"Let 'em go!" roared Zer.

Nathan looked down. Zer was sitting in the water, cursing the team and the people at the Crossroads. Nathan asked, "You hurt?"

"Leg!" said Zer.

Nathan helped him up. They were knee-deep in the cold water, and Zer leaned heavily on him. They made their way to the bank. The team was still thrashing along upstream, but the drag of the wrecked wagon had slowed them down considerably.

"Leg broke?" asked Nathan.

" 'Feared so. Heard the damn' thing go when I lit in the riffle." Galloping horses were coming down the road. Mat Foley's voice: "Zer! Where in hell are you?"

"Down here!" Nathan shouted.

He went through the brush to the road. The sky was beginning to lighten in the east, and Mat Foley was pulling up the black stallion. Behind him, strung out along the road, were Bert and Joe.

"Where's Zer?" Mat demanded.

Nathan pointed. "Broken leg."

Mat looked down. "How about you?"

Nathan shrugged. "Wet," he said.

CHAPTER XII

BLOODY HARPE AND WOMAN CLAYDON, HAVING found no more victims, traveled the Trace back to Natchez, a town of luxury and vice perched on a bluff overlooking the Mississippi River. Here wealthy planters came to get supplies, to spend their money, to buy slaves, to hear the news and find out whether they belonged to Spain or the United States—or perhaps England or France. The streets, muddy after the drizzle, held a few wide-tired wagons that had come down the river on flatboats (for the Trace from Nashville was not wide enough to be used as a road, and only horseback or foot traffic was found on it), and there was an occasional cabriolet drawn by spanking blooded horses imported from France. But all in all, it was a sleepy town, for its revelries lasted long, and the partakers seldom stirred much before noon.

Harpe and Claydon rode their blaze-faced horses in silence, watching everything, Harpe with that perpetual scowl on his heavy face and no hat on his head, Claydon with his fat face apparently blank but with his small black eyes probing everywhere—especially when a woman appeared.

They took the steep path down to the shelf that held Natchez-Under-the-Hill, the rendezvous for river boatmen and all the lawless, the home of saloons, a ragged band of Choctaw Indians, and women of all prices.

They tied their horses to a hitch rail near the Mississippi Mud Saloon, and went inside.

The ceiling was low and swirled with tobacco smoke

that almost smothered the whale-oil lamp hanging from the ceiling, so that its yellow flame was feeble and offered little illumination. A reed organ was wheezing, and a black-haired Spanish girl sang a husky song in her strange language. Claydon didn't know the words, but they were sad and haunting. He looked at the girl and began to feel tight inside.

"Rye," said Harpe.

Claydon turned quickly on the balls of his feet. He was fast for a man of two hundred and forty pounds. "Got any brandy?"

"Sure.

Claydon was no fancy drinker. He tossed off four glasses of peach brandy as fast as they could be poured. He felt it spread into his blood, and he turned around toward the Spanish girl.

"Whatever you do, don't flash that money. You make too big a show, and old Sam Mason will have our heads."

"Wait for me," said Claydon, his blood pounding as he started for the girl.

"You like Carmenita?" the bartender asked with a leer. Woman Claydon didn't answer. He didn't even turn his head. She had black hair and eyes and a chunky build—and she was a woman.

He heard Harpe's voice somewhere in the back of his mind: "I ain't waiting. I got business of my own. I'll meet you here in the morning."

Carmenita was an agreeable girl, especially when she saw a couple of gold quadruple-piaster pieces.

For once he was exhausted when he met Harpe the next morning. They had a drink, and Harpe growled, "Old Mason moved back across this side of the river."

"What for?" asked Claydon.

"Spanish soldiers looking for people without passports on the other side. And maybe," he said thoughtfully, "he figured to check up on some of us."

Claydon reached for the brandy. "For what?" he asked without meeting Harpe's glowering eyes.

"Maybe he wonders if we're turnin' in everything we take along the Trace."

Claydon killed the drink, wondering if Harpe suspected anything. He set down the glass and looked sharply at Harpe, but Harpe's eyes were not on him. Claydon took another drink. If Harpe suspected anything, he'd wait for Claydon to go back after his caches, and then—it might be best to kill Harpe first. But there was no hurry; Harpe was smart enough to know the stuff would be permanently lost if he killed Claydon too soon.

Claydon was still rolling that over in his mind when Harpe said: "Drink up. We better start along the riverbank to find Mason."

"What'll we tell him when we find him?"

Harpe shrugged. "Tell him what happened. We got a horse out of them three whipsawers—and that's all."

"How about the boat?"

Harpe glared at him. "Sam Mason don't know nothin' about that boat."

"I wish we could make a stake." Claydon pretended to shiver. "I don't like this cold country."

Harpe sneered. "Always lookin' for a hot country and hot-blooded wimmen."

"It ain't all that."

"What is it?"

Claydon began his usual complaint about the percentages. Besides being something that irked him, it always diverted Harpe. "You get a third, I get a third—"

"Old Mason's spies tell us when somebody's comin'."

"It don't add up to me. I figure—"

"You gents goin' to headquarters?"

Claydon spun around. Harpe was only a little behind him.

The newcomer laughed boisterously.

"Brooks," said Claydon, relieved.

The newcomer nodded, a tall, hard-faced but good-looking man whose eyes were always roaming. He pushed up to the bar between them and poured a glass of peach brandy. "I just got run back from Fort Concordia," he said. "The Spanish are right hostile."

"Know where Mason is?" asked Harpe.

Brooks gestured up and down the river. "Not far. He doesn't want to leave Natchez." Brooks poured another. "It's perfect here. Glass handles his stuff. Governor Claiborne hasn't got enough soldiers to find him, and lots of travelers are coming up from New Orleans with money."

"You have any luck this trip?" asked Harpe.

Brooks made an ugly face. "All the information was wrong." Claydon was silent. Brooks had told that story before.

"Let's hit the trail," said Harpe. "There's caves up and down the river."

"I'd say down."

Harpe shook his heavy head. "Up around Rocky Springs."

They slept out that night near the Trace, and found Mason's camp the next afternoon, in a limestone cave a couple of miles off the road. They put their horses out to browse in the cane, and climbed the trail.

Thomas Mason and John Mason were there, and

Marguerite, John's wife, was roasting a bear ham inside the cave. Samuel Mason got to his feet. He was about fifty-five years old, tall and fine-featured, and weighed about two hundred pounds. He looked hale and hearty, dressed in leather hunting shirt with moccasins and long leggings. Only one bad feature marred his good looks: a large tooth that projected from his upper jaw.

"How much?" he asked Harpe.

"That last bunch wasn't in very good shape. They had mighty little gold, but we took their horse and sold it to Glass."

Old Mason looked at him. "One horse?"

"They was whipsawin'."

"How much did you get from Glass?"

"Twenty piasters."

"Then the horse must have been worth sixty."

"A good horse," said Harpe, pulling a leather bag from the wallet of his shirt. "Here's eighteen piasters. Claydon and me spent a couple under the hill."

"Leaves eighteen. That's six apiece." He looked sharply at Claydon. "Better than nothing, eh?"

For a moment Claydon was scared. He thought old Mason was onto them. But Mason, sitting cross-legged on the rock shelf in front of the cave, casually divided the silver coins into three piles and pushed one to each of them.

Claydon took a moment to admire Harpe's smartness in seeming to account so scrupulously. The man was no fool, for all of his ready murderousness.

Then Harpe revealed another of his shrewd ideas. He pulled a piece of paper from under his belt and handed it to Mason. "See what that says?"

Mason looked it over, reading slowly. At first he frowned, but then he roared with laughter. "Nine

119

hundred dollars for the two of us! They want us, eh, Setton?"

"They want us bad," said Harpe.

Mason looked up, narrow-eyed. "What's this about you bein' Harpe? You aren't, are you?"

Harpe shook his ugly head. "Not me. You know my name. I was John Taylor when I joined up with you, and you wanted my name changed to Setton."

Mason tried hard to cover the projecting tooth with his lip. "You look pretty much like the description of Harpe."

Harpe made no effort to smile or pass it off. "Harpe was killed in Kentucky years ago."

Mason tossed the small circular aside and turned suddenly to Brooks. "How about you?"

"No luck," said Brooks. "My party was broke."

Mason stared at him without a change in his face, but his eyes grew cold. "That's three times in a row," he said. He pulled out his pistol and shot the man between the eyes. Brooks's pistol was in his hand, but his finger never touched the trigger. Without a sound, he fell over backward and a little to one side.

Mason grinned wolfishly. "Git a rope on his feet and drag him out," he said.

Claydon glanced sidewise. Harpe's hand was on his tomahawk, but as Mason grinned and thrust the empty pistol into his belt, Harpe's hand dropped away from the weapon.

Claydon, watching both of them, wondered if Mason knew the man was Harpe. It was hard to say, for one never knew what was going on in Mason's head, and Harpe denied his own name convincingly.

They dragged the body into the woods, and toward dark Mason's other sons, Samuel, Jr., and Magnus, about

120

seventeen and sixteen, came in from the Trace also reporting poor luck.

After supper, Mason, his stomach full, got out a demijohn of whisky and lay back against the rock wall. "We might as well face it," he said. "These here fellers comin' up the Trace these days aren't very good game. We been workin' the Trace so long, a lot of fellers with money take a boat from New Orleans to Philadelphia. We got to work out a different system." He had a long drink. "Our best bet," he said, "is to tackle the flatboats on their way down. We can take what money they've got, and we can always sell the goods to Tony Glass."

"You can't handle that from here," said Harpe casually. "It's too far from the river."

"We'll move tomorrow. I've got a cave right where I can watch the river, and I've got spies in Nogales and Little Prairie. They'll report when anybody shows money."

"How'll you capture the stuff?"

"Row out in small boats and tell them we're stranded and want to buy rifles and gunpowder." His lip slowly peeled back over the projecting tooth. "So we take their cargoes, and get our money back besides."

"It's not as easy as handlin' gold."

"Takes a little more organization," said Mason. "We'll have to have crews to take the boats on to Natchez and all—but the volume is big. Sometimes there's twenty boats a day come down the river—and there'll be more, now that the U.S. has bought Louisiana.

"What makes you think so?" asked Harpe.

"Lots of people in the Western Country will move lock, stock, and barrel to a new country where land is free. Some will settle in Louisiana, some will go on to

121

the Tejas Country. At any rate, they'll carry every sou they've got in the world—and that makes good pickin's."

"What about this reward money?" asked Harpe.

"What about it? Can anybody find us in the canebrake? And if they could find us, have they got the guts to try to capture us? Nah, they run like sheep!"

Nine hundred dollars, thought Claydon. Nine hundred for the two of them. He looked at Mason and then at Harpe, speculating.

CHAPTER XIII

BACK IN THE STATE OF FOLEY, ZER SAT IN MAT'S cabin with his broken leg splinted and laid across a chair. Martha had not come down because nobody had gone to notify her. Old Mat sat at the table drinking whisky.

"And not a damn' shot fired hit man or beast," he growled. "So there's nothing we could go to court about."

Nathan said, "No jury in this part of the country would give you a verdict against Bill Brandon."

Mat asked abruptly, "How do you know it was Bill Brandon?"

Nathan met his eyes. "I assumed it was," he said.

"I don't like assuming," said Mat.

Nathan replied stiffly, "You assumed that Pete Brandon had no right to ride through this valley."

Mat roared up. "I tell you this is my valley!"

Nathan refused to get excited. "Can you stay in this valley forever? Haven't you got to take corn out to sell, and go outside to get supplies?"

"We'll go back to doing everything by hand."

"How would you make an ax by hand? There's no iron in the valley, no sugar, no salt, no coffee."

"We can do without them things," Bert Foley said quietly.

"And we can grow our own tobacco," said Joe.

Nathan looked at them both. "What about gunpowder?"

"I know how to make powder," said Mat.

"It takes sulphur and charcoal and saltpeter," Nathan

reminded him. "You can make charcoal, but you can't make sulphur and you can't make lead for balls."

"He's right," Zer said, nursing his drink.

"You agin me too?" Mat demanded.

"There's no use bein' blind."

The hard-faced Peggy came in the front door. "Bert, you better come up to the cabin," she said.

Bert looked up, alert. "What's the matter?"

"There's a fire in the haystack. We been fightin' it all morning."

Bert got up. "You get Ben to help you?"

"That coward, Ben Metheny, wouldn't help nobody!" Her cynical eyes narrowed like a man's. "He heard them shots and he's been holed up in his cabin ever since. The son-of-a—" She glanced at Mat's wife, back in the corner. "He's afraid he'll have to do some work," she ended.

"I'll go with you," said Joe, and they walked out together. Peggy addressed Mat, and it was the first time Nathan had ever heard her do it directly. "You better do something about this or we'll all wind up in an early grave."

"They can't hurt us," said Mat.

"Like hell they can't! In another two months the woods will be dry. What if a fire gets started in a stiff wind?"

Mat glared at her. She glared back, then stalked out and started walking back up the creek.

Nathan went to the door. "I'll get your buggy," he told Zer, "and get you home. Mine's smashed to kindling wood."

Zer shook his head. "I'll bed down right here. Martha—with me in this shape—" He shook his head.

Mat took a swallow of rye. "At that, she ain't like

124

Nancy."

"Better if she was."

"There's nothin' worse than a woman with a tongue floppin' in the middle."

"There's something just as bad," said Zer. "A woman who won't even talk civil."

It was the first time Nathan had ever heard Zer discuss his family affairs. He watched Zer take a big drink of whisky. Then he pulled open the door and went outside.

The sun was high, and he saw a buzzard, far down the creek, slanting down in a long glide to bring it to the dead horse. He scanned the edge of the forest on the left side all the way up to his own place, but saw nothing. And he guessed he never would.

He took the long walk up the creek. Then he crossed over and went to help Bert and Joe carry water to the haystack. Peggy was carrying too, but the big wooden buckets were heavy for her. Tim came down and joined them, but the stack was too far from the creek, and all the water they could get up the steep path was not more than enough to wet the hay and make it smolder.

Nathan said, "We might as well fork it apart, let the middle burn, and save the rest."

"Expect you're right," said Bert.

They got it apart and opened up the middle so that the fire would burn out. By then it was noon.

"You better come in and feed up," said Peggy.

"Thanks, no. I left before sunup this morning, and I imagine Sarah heard the shooting, and she'll be wondering about me." He rather liked Peggy. For all her cynicism she seemed the best of the bunch except Alice and Sarah. Katherine was strange, but he guessed she couldn't be anything else with Ben Metheny. Martha

125

was never friendly to anybody, and Joe's wife, Thelma, was standoffish and suspicious.

Nathan smiled at Peggy and went back down the hill and across the creek.

Sarah was waiting for him at the door. She put her arms around him and held him tight. He lifted her face and saw tears, then pulled her head against his chest and patted her. "Everything's all right," he said soothingly.

"Did anybody—"

"Zer got a broken leg when the wagon turned over. Not too bad, I guess. Maybe a small bone close to the ankle. He'll be all right in a few days."

"But nobody got hit with a bullet?"

"No, I don't think they aimed to hit anybody. Got anything to eat?" he asked.

"Corn dodgers and hominy grits and fat pork."

"Sounds good," said Nathan.

That afternoon the wind shifted to the top of the valley and blew straight down the creek. Nathan scanned the sky for clouds. "Looks like good weather," he said.

"We need rain."

"We'll get it," he said with assurance. "Spring's a long way off yet.

He made the rounds carefully that night, saw that the horse-pen gate was tight, ran the hogs into the barn, secured the chickens, and on final thought put the dogs into the barn also. He stood at the front door of the cabin, smoking a last crooked cigar, quietly watching the stars and listening to the night noises. Sarah came out and stood beside him, soundlessly, and they both watched and listened but heard nothing out of place—an occasional cluck from a sleepy chicken, crickets down in the meadow, bullfrogs along the creek.

126

Nathan finished his cigar, tossed the end to the ground, and stepped on it with his moccasin. That made him think: he needed a pair of shoepacks for winter—at least before it started raining—but the way it looked now he would have to do his own cobbling.

Sarah half whispered, "It's peaceful tonight."

Nathan awoke sometime after midnight, eyes suddenly wide open, brain alert, sniffing smoke. He jumped out of bed and into his leggings and moccasins.

Sarah was up beside him, moving quickly, quietly. He snatched his rifle from the deer horns and, in the dark, poured powder in the priming pan. He opened the door and stepped out, moving to one side.

The moon, about to go down behind the western ridge, shed a weird light over the valley. He went around the cabin and made a quick circuit of his horse pen and barn. The horses were nervous, tossing their heads, making quick trots from one side of the pen to another. The dogs in the barn were growling.

Nathan came back to the front of the cabin, puzzled. "The valley looks strange," Sarah observed. "Almost like—fog." Nathan stared. Then he looked back at the mountain behind them and sniffed. "That's burning brush and timber," he said. "Lots of green stuff in it, just dry enough to burn. Wind picks up the smoke and carries it over the mountain and down into the valley."

"Then it's burning on the other side."

"Must be."

"I wonder how it got started."

He hesitated. "Lightning, maybe."

"There's been no storm."

He looked down at her. "No. No storm."

She coughed. "I think I'd better go in, Nate."

"The smoke won't be as bad inside."

"What are *you* going to do, Nate?"

"I'm going down the valley."

He met Tim and Alice just as the moon was going down. Tim looked at the ridges and asked worriedly, "Do you think—"

"Just living in a valley full of smoke never hurt anybody."

Nathan wasn't entirely right in that conclusion, as he realized three days later. Used to the pure air that generally swept through the valley, its inhabitants had difficulty getting adjusted to the smoke. Three days later the smoke was much thicker, and all were beginning to cough. At night the Metheny kids filled the whole valley with their whooping. On the third day they met at Mat's, red-eyed, short-tempered, pursued everywhere by the smoke. Only Nathan and George McGee were fairly free, for their places, at the upper end of the valley, and both near the timber, were not as much affected as the others.

Mat said belligerently, "If they did it, I'll have their scalps."

"You'll never prove it," said Zer.

"They haven't burned anything of yours—even timber," Nathan pointed out.

"This valley is mine, isn't it!" Mat roared. "Not the mountain up there."

Zer hobbled to the window with a cane whittled from hickory. "Anybody been up there?"

"Tim and I were up yesterday," said Nathan.

Zer coughed. "What did you find?"

"A creeping ground-fire on the other side, headed for the top of the mountain. It's burning slow, and so far has covered a strip about a half a mile wide."

"Any sign of how it started?"

"Not that we could tell."

"It could be an accident," said Zer as he hobbled back to the jug, "and it could be on purpose."

Alice came in. "Tim!" Her voice was filled with fright. "Tommy's got a coughing spasm," she said.

Tim spun around. Alice's eyes, like those of everybody else, were rimmed with red.

Mat's wife came out of her corner. "Honey and onions," she said. "I'll go with you."

For a moment there was silence. Bert Foley moved to close the door, and through the swirls of smoke came the racking cough of a small boy.

Zer, with the cup to his mouth, stared through the window. Mat got to his feet. "I'm goin' into the Crossroads."

Zer looked at him. "I don't think you better."

Mat roared. "Who in hell d'you think you are! My own son tellin' me what to do!" He glared at Zer and stamped to the door. "Abraham!" he shouted. "Harness up the light wagon!"

"Yas, suh," came the answer out of the smoke.

Mat went to the storeroom and came back with an ax. "I call you to witness, I'm takin' no firearms."

"What's the ax for?" asked Zer.

"To clear logs off the road." Mat grinned. "But I doubt I'll need it. I'm drivin' down the creek."

Zer nodded. "It can be done."

They stood outside. Tim's small boy was still coughing. Mat tossed the ax under the seat and stepped up on the wheel hub. "When I come back," he said, "I'll have supplies."

They watched him drive off, saw him leave the road

and push the team through the brush, and a moment later, after the crackling of dead branches, they heard the splash of water.

Nathan said soberly, "We shouldn't have let him go alone."

Zer's comment was derisive. "When are you gonna learn to be yourself? You can't run around wet-nursin' Mat the rest of your life—and you're no Ben Metheny or George McGee."

Nathan looked around. George was fifty feet away, studying the smoke, but he had heard his name, for now he turned.

Nathan frowned, confused by a moment of self-doubt. Why did he stick so tight? Was he like Ben and George, trying to get his fingers on a piece of Mat's land?

Joe Foley looked worried. "I hear somebody choppin' wood."

They listened, and then turned to face downstream. The sharp, clear strokes of an ax came up the valley.

"That's the way Mat chops, all right—and it sounds like he's mad," said Zer.

"We better go help," said Bert. "His one arm is still lame."

"He's all right," Zer answered. "Long as he's choppin' wood he ain't in no trouble."

Mat returned in the late afternoon. They saw him coming up the road, driving the team and walking behind. He was cussing a blue streak. "Damn' fools!" he said. "They dropped a log over the creek around every bend. I cut through eight of 'em before I gave up."

"Where's the wagon?" asked Zer.

Mat drove alongside and turned the team over to Abraham. "Didn't have room to turn around, account of the rocks. I unhitched the team and left the wagon be."

"That makes three wagons we lost so far."

Mat stomped up and down, his great square back seeming to acquire more authority and more power as he cursed the people at the Crossroads: old man Fairfax, the one-armed Carr at the livery stable, Elisha Wilson, Jim Sigler and, above all, Bill Brandon.

Zer turned to look at the mountain. His and Martha's only child was buried up there, among four other Foley graves.

The next day Mat's wife fixed honey and onions for all the children in the valley. The dogs had taken to digging under houses and barns. The horses were nervous, and they had to watch them carefully in the meadow or keep them penned up and feed them corn. Three of Metheny's broke loose and headed for the narrows below Mat's place. Mat and Abraham stopped two of them, but the third one bolted and got away, and Mat on his big black stallion couldn't get close to him before he reached a place in the road where somebody had dropped fresh logs over it. Ben's horse jumped the first one, but Mat came back snorting. "No sense risking the stallion over them logs. It wasn't a very good horse anyway."

Nathan went on up to his cabin. The smoke was so thick up there he could hardly see from one corner of the cabin to the other. Inside, it was almost as bad. Sarah, red-eyed, was wearing a blue handkerchief over her mouth. "The smoke made me sick," she said. "I had to do something."

Nathan sat on the ground outside that night, his back against the cabin by the side of the door. He smoked a cigar while Sarah sat in the doorway beside him. The moon came up red and bloody-looking.

"You aren't helping much with your cigars," she noted.

He heard the amusement in her voice. He blew tobacco smoke into the fog of wood smoke, and said, "Making a little backfire of my own."

"It's six days now," Sarah noted. "Surely—" She left it unfinished.

Surely nothing—and she knew it as well as he did.

The next day the smoke thinned out until Nathan could see all the cabins in the valley. Nathan breathed the fresh air and saddled the gelding to go down to Mat's.

Halfway down the valley he picked up Tim. Ben Metheny, across the creek, was doggedly chopping away at a pile of wood, and refused to look up.

Tim studied the horses around the cabin. "Zer and Joe and Bert are already here," he noted.

Nathan said slowly, "Isn't that a white flag up at the edge of the timber?"

Tim studied it. There was still some smoke—enough to make a haze—but he nodded. "It sure is. Probably an ultimatum."

"Let's get down there and tell Mat." Nathan booted the gelding into a gallop.

Zer was holding the door open as Nathan dismounted. "There's a white flag up at the edge of the timber," Nathan told Mat.

Mat drank a full cup of whisky. "To hell with 'em. They started this. Let's see if they can finish it."

Zer hobbled to the table. He was walking better now, but he still trod lightly on the game leg. "You better go, Mat—and go unarmed," he said heavily.

Mat looked up. Mat's eyes, too, were rimmed with fire. "When my own kin turns agin me, I might as well,"

132

he said heavily. Nobody answered.

Mat got up and went to the door. He still had the tapered build of a fighter—big across the shoulders, slim in the hips. He was light on his feet, once he got up. He stepped outside and began to walk slowly uphill toward the piece of white cloth spread on the low limb of an oak tree.

A figure came out from behind the tree. "Come unarmed!" Bill Brandon roared down.

Mat stopped. It must have been hard for him to do, for he turned to the men in the door for encouragement. But nobody said a word or made a move. Mat took the pistol out of his belt and tossed it to the group. Bert caught it and took it inside, and Nathan heard him lay it on the table.

Now a second man came from behind the tree—Carr, the liveryman.

Mat stopped and bellowed: "Two on one! You aim to fight that way, Brandon?"

It was merely a point of carping with Mat, for Nathan knew he would not have hesitated to take on both men in an open fight—Carr having but one arm anyway.

Brandon called down, "Bring Nate with you."

Zer looked at Nathan, who went out to join Mat, and both men walked slowly uphill as Brandon and Carr came down. They were still fifty feet apart when Mat demanded, "What do you mean by trespassing on my land?"

Brandon stopped. "Do you want to talk or don't you?"

It was a poor spot for Mat to bluff, for Brandon had all the cards. Nathan looked at Brandon. The man's jowls weren't as heavy as they had been. There was an ominous look about his face, and a hardness in his eyes

133

that Nathan had not seen there before.

Mat glared at him, then grunted and resumed climbing. They faced each other a moment later, Mat with an appearance of bafflement that was more like that of outraged royalty than anything Nathan could think of, and Brandon with that deadly look in his face.

"You been settin' fires to run me out," Mat said. "We aim to do the talkin'—not you."

Mat swore, and Brandon waited until he finished.

"We fought the Revolution against a king that arrested people for walkin' in his forests," Brandon said coldly. "Do you figger to set yourself up here as a king?"

"It's my land. I—"

"I want to tell you this, Mat Foley: the grand jury couldn't indict anybody for killin' my kid—but he's dead, shot in the back."

"He—"

Brandon's voice rang out suddenly. "Shut up, Foley, and listen, or else go back to your place and wait!"

Knots were forming and unforming in Mat's jaw.

Brandon went on: "We had a meetin', us people at the Crossroads, and we decided the Foleys was gettin' too big for their britches. So we agreed on one thing. We're goin' to run the whole damn' pack of you out of Kentucky. We've got no place here for kings and the king's forests and the king's deer."

"Run us out of Kentucky! That's robbery!"

"It wasn't when *you* did it."

"This ain't Injun country," said Mat. "You can't take a man's land away from him." He added, in a last flash of defiance, "You haven't got enough on your side."

"We've got enough," said Brandon, "but we don't want your land—and that's what I came to talk about."

134

"What do you want, then?"

"Just what I said, Mat Foley. *We want you and all the damn' red Foleys in your outfit out of Kentucky!*"

Mat frowned. "You want to make me an offer for my valley?" Nathan knew there wasn't enough cash within fifty miles of the Crossroads to buy the valley.

But Brandon said: "There's a land speculator at the Falls. You and one man can go out on horseback, and nobody will bother you. They say this feller pays a fair price, and we'll give you a chance to sell—on one condition: that you're out of this valley within a week after you get back from the Falls."

Nathan could see Mat's neck begin to thicken, and he waited for an outburst.

"How do I know you haven't told it all over that you're runnin' me out?"

"I don't give a damn whether you know it or not. That's the offer. Take it or leave it."

Mat glared at him for a long time, but Brandon yielded nothing. At last Mat said heavily, "We'll start in the morning."

Brandon said, "You and one man."

Without another word Mat turned on his heel and started back to the cabin. As Brandon watched him go, he said to Nathan in a low voice, "I always figgered you had some guts of your own, Nate. How long are you goin' to string along with that old bull? I never figgered you that way, Nate."

"What way?" asked Nate, puzzled.

"The kind that would lick a man's boots to git a piece of his land when he dies."

Nathan's eyes narrowed. "If I thought you meant that, Brandon—"

Carr spoke up. "It's what everybody is sayin', Nate."

135

"I married Sarah, and—"

"Some people think maybe you married Mat."

Nathan felt his face turning red. He moistened his lips. "A man has to settle his own affairs," he said stiffly, and went back downhill.

Mat was drinking and talking out his vehemence in angry words. They let him talk for a while. His wife sat in the corner, separating flax fibers from the hulls, throwing the hulls in a wooden bucket, and laying the fibers in a neat stack on the floor. Mat shouted, "Ma, we need another jug!" She got up and pulled a demijohn of rye from under the bed. As she carried it across the floor, it seemed almost too much for her frail arms, but she placed the jug on the table and went back to her corner. Mat went on, vengefully, bitterly, until he was talked out.

Finally Zer asked, "Who's goin' with you?"

"What do you mean?"

"You've got no choice," said Zer. "They offered you a fair way out. You got a chance to sell before the whole country knows what's goin' on. I say you better sell now before the price drops by half."

"I won't be run out of my valley."

"What about the Spanish country you're always talkin' about? With what you could get out of this valley you could buy a million acres down there and set up a grant where you would be the boss of everything."

Mat's eyes burned as he watched Zer, and it was not hard to know what he was thinking. Zer had made an appeal Mat couldn't resist; in addition, it gave him a way out.

"I'll take Bert with me," Mat announced decisively. "You stay here and take care of the valley, Zer."

Nathan and Sarah, standing at their own place, watched Mat and Bert take the lower trail over the north ridge at sunup the next morning.

Sarah asked, "Do you think he'll be able to sell at a good price?"

"Depends," said Nathan. He went inside and got a cigar, lit it with a coal from the fireplace, and came back out. There was a little mist in the valley that morning, but it was disappearing under the rays of the sun. Nathan sat on the ground, his back against the cabin.

"You're pretty serious, Nate."

"I was just thinking."

"About Mat?"

"About Mat—and us."

"What about us?"

"This valley is all Mat's—every foot of it."

"Yes."

"I mean it's in his name."

"I suppose so."

Nathan motioned with the cigar. "And all this stuff—the cabin, the land, the barns, the stock, the crops, even the harness and the hay—everything belongs to Mat."

"We're all one family, aren't we?"

He studied her. "Should we be?"

"I don't know what you're trying to say, Nate."

"Mat had a lot of brothers and sisters, didn't he?"

"Twelve, all told."

He looked at his cigar. "But they didn't all stay together."

"No. Only one—his older sister Sarah, the one I was named after—stayed with Mat. She was sick, and I hardly remember her. She's buried up on the mountain there."

"I was wondering," he said, "why Mat is so

determined to keep the family all together."

"The land is Mat's. It's only natural that he'd want us to stay on it."

"Maybe—but is it natural that we should do so?"

"We're his children, aren't we?"

Nathan looked up at her. "Looks to me like you're a grown woman."

She blushed and sat down beside him, her heavy gray dress covering her legs.

"When a man's old enough to be married," he said, "he's supposed to go out and get a place of his own."

"It isn't necessary when we've already got a good place."

He smoked for a while. Down the creek the mist was gone. Chickens were clucking over scraps. A hundred wild pigeons whirred up out of a tree on the north ridge, and the beat of their wings was lost in the still air.

"Have you ever seen any of your other uncles and aunts?"

"Only Aunt Sarah."

"And she was sick?"

"She hardly ever got out of bed after she came to the valley."

"Where are the others?"

"Scattered all over the world, I guess."

"Isn't it odd that of all the twelve, only Aunt Sarah, who was an invalid, came to see Mat?"

"They were all too busy, I suppose."

He sat there for a while and smoked his cigar.

"How long will they be gone?" she asked.

"Six or seven days."

She touched his arm. "You're not worried about the property, are you?"

"No, I'm not worried about the property."

138

"It's all in the family anyway, so it doesn't make any difference, does it, Nate?"

He looked down the valley and drew a deep breath. "I don't know," he said.

After a while she said, "What about Mother, Nate?"

For a second he was startled. Then he asked, "What about her?"

She didn't answer, and he looked down at her, but her eyes were on the ground. He sat for a moment, thinking, the sun warm on his thighs. "I never heard anybody worry about her before," he said finally.

"That's what hurts, Nate." Sarah's words began to come rapidly. "Nobody ever thinks about Mother. Mat never asks her what she wants to do. You'd think she was a slave." A tear fell on the rough gray material of her dress. "Mother came here and raised seven children in this valley—buried two. She worked like a man, but Mat never once asked her opinion about anything. She never speaks. She never raises her eyes. She—she's like a walking corpse."

Nate took the cigar from his mouth. "I know all that, but I don't know what to do about it."

"Who knows what she thinks or what she wants?" Sarah went on. She was near to tears.

"I don't—"

But Sarah was determined to have her say. "She's not young any more, Nate. What will happen in Tejas, with all the terribly hard work of a new country? I don't believe she can stand it, Nate."

He drew a short puff on the cigar. "You got an answer?" he asked. She was crying freely now, and he put an arm around her shoulders.

"I don't know," she sobbed. "She won't live long in another pioneer country—but I don't know."

He stared at Mat's cabin down the valley. Eliza and Mat's wife were doing the wash, and the sound of the battling paddles was clear and sharp in the morning air. Nate himself wondered how much longer Mat's wife could do the heavy work of a farm household, and he wondered uncomfortably what Mat would do when she could not. But more than anything he wondered what she thought. Was she an automaton, as she seemed to be, without reaction or feeling, or had she once felt resentment and offered resistance, only to be beaten down by Mat's superior force? Nate frowned as he looked down the valley, and thought back, trying to recall whether he had ever seen her raise her eyes.

CHAPTER XIV

FOR SEVERAL DAYS THERE WAS NO TROUBLE. THOUGH the wind shifted back to the southwest, the fire on the other side of the mountain was burned out, and the valley did not again fill with smoke. The sun shone warm and bright, and Nathan, mending harness in the lee of the barn while he listened to the hum of the spinning wheel from the cabin, began to feel easy in his mind, although he reminded himself that their respite was only temporary.

Mat Foley returned in mid-afternoon of the sixth day. Nathan heard a hail from down the valley, and looked up to see Mat on his big black stallion and Bert on a dun horse riding down the steep slope from the opposite ridge.

Nathan dropped his awl and thread and went to the cabin. Sarah was cracking chestnuts to put in a stew. "Mat's back," he told her. "We'd better go down, I think, and find out the answer."

He rode the bay gelding at a walk, with Sarah clinging on behind. All over the valley the Foleys were gathering. Across the creek, Nancy McGee was giving some last shrill-voiced instructions to their six children.

"Nancy always did talk too loud," said Sarah.

And too much, Nathan thought, but he kept it to himself.

The gaunt-faced Martha set out across the meadow afoot. Zer was already down at the cabin, leaning on his cane. The wispy-haired Katherine and her husband, Ben, were sufficiently concerned this time to attend, Nathan noticed. Bert's wife, Peggy, was under a hickory

141

tree, shading her eyes with her hand, and she alone was making no effort to join the movement down the valley. Nathan was surprised to find himself disappointed. They picked up Alice and Tim. Alice, though she was older than Sarah, was enough like her to have been a twin—and sometimes they were called twins, for they had both been born on the same date, four years apart. Tim, younger than any of them, looked considerably worried.

Joe and Thelma, both too fat, were walking across the meadow and angling down toward Mat's place.

They crowded into the cabin—all of the Foley grownups but Peggy. The women sat on two bearskins; the men sat at the table and on the floor. Mat's wife was in her corner, churning tirelessly, her eyes on the floor, and Nate wondered how she summoned enough strength to her frail arms to move the dasher up and down.

Mat, with a week's grizzled red beard on his big face, waited until all were in; then he looked up, and he could no longer restrain himself. "We're all going to the Tejas Country," he announced. "It's settled."

Nobody answered for a moment. Then the women began to murmur. Mat looked pleased. "We leave one week from today," he said, and slammed the table with his big fist. "We'll have a kingdom of our own in New Spain! All Foleys—every golblasted one. The Spanish government gives grants to people who can work the soil, and they're cryin' for people to settle."

"How much land can we get?" asked Zer.

"Thirty-six thousand acres."

"Can you pay for that much?"

"Paying is the easiest part. Ten cents an acre or so after the first few years. It's heads of families that count. Every head of a family gets so much, and the man who gets the grant is the impresario—boss of the whole thing. We got eight families. With all rights we're good for a bigger piece of land than anybody in the whole damned State of Kentucky—and this time it'll *be* the State of Foley!"

There was deep silence for a moment except for the steady chug of the churn. Then Zer said: "It takes money to run a place like that. How much did you get for the valley?"

Mat grinned until he looked like Satan himself. "I sold the valley, kit and caboodle, for $60,000!"

Joe Foley whistled. George McGee's little eyes were black pools. Even Martha's customary reserve did not entirely hold in the face of such an enormous amount of money.

"Sight unseen!" Mat roared.

Nathan frowned. Mat was feeling his oats, but that was only natural. He had made a deal that would put money into his hands such as nobody in Kentucky had ever seen—not many, anyway. It was natural for Mat to feel like crowing.

"What do we keep?" asked Zer.

"One wagon apiece, twelve saddle horses, personal property—rifles, axes, plows, harness, three blacks all told. The rest go with the valley, for I hear there's some doubt about the slaves in Spanish territory."

"What are you goin' to use to pull the wagons?"

"Oxen. I've got sixty head on the way out here now. They'll be here in three, four days. The first thing we've got to do is get loaded. We'll want corn, salt, sugar, coffee, gunpowder and lead, dried meat and fruit, seed, tar buckets, everything we need to set up in a virgin country."

Nathan asked slowly, "Do you know exactly where to go in New Spain?"

143

Mat straightened belligerently. "We go through Natchitoches and report at Nacogdoches. They may send us on to Bejar to pick out the actual location. But down there," he went on, "it's always summer."

"There are still Indians too—Apaches and Comanches."

"There were Indians in Kentucky when I came here."

Nathan was turning it over in his mind. "Is there any way you can be sure of getting land down there before we leave the United States?"

Mat answered him with an air of exaggerated patience. "I talked to a dozen men. Every one had been to New Orleans and back, and they all say the same thing: Spain wants good hard-working settlers. They want to develop the country. It's good land, fertile, lots of water, warm climate. They want to populate it. All we have to do is take an oath of allegiance to the Spanish government."

Nathan paced the floor a time or two. "The crops will be different from our crops in Kentucky."

"Certainly they will—but we're farmers, aren't we? It's land—and stuff grows on it. The gover'ment down there wants you to plant and grow."

"I hear they keep a tight rein on trade, make you buy certain things from certain places, put on a lot of taxes—tithes for the Church."

All eyes were on Nathan now, as he began to present another side of the picture. "We'd all have to be Catholics, too."

Mat roared. "What the hell! My family was all Catholics. I was raised a Catholic!"

Nathan looked at him calmly. "*I* was raised a Methodist," he said.

Mat hit the table with his big hand, and the demijohn

quivered. "It's all the same God, isn't it? What's the difference what church you go to?"

Nathan looked at Sarah and saw the worry in her blue eyes. He had been about to answer, but decided not to. He walked to the door. A white flag was hanging from the oak tree. He turned back to Mat. "You better send somebody up there to tell them your plans."

Mat jumped to his feet. "By God, I won't be forced!"

Nathan said mildly: "They aren't forcing you. They just want to know the answer. And you've already made up your mind. You might as well tell them so they'll let you alone while you're getting ready to move."

"That's right," said Zer. "Might as well let 'em know. I don't want to live in smoke for the next week."

Mat sat down, glowering. "All right," he growled. "Joe, go up there and tell 'em we're leaving a week from today. And tell 'em to go to hell, with my compliments."

The fat son of old Mat got to his feet. Nathan understood why Mat was sending Joe: Joe was the least capable of giving trouble, and everybody in the country knew it. As Joe went out of the door and began to cross the meadow, Bill Brandon walked down to meet him.

Mat said, "Zer, I want you to organize a crew of three men, take half a dozen horses, and clear the logs off the road so we can get out."

Zer nodded.

Mat's wife stopped her churning. She did not even lift the lid, but seemed to know, without looking, that the butter was made. She picked up the heavy churn, holding it against her stomach, and went out. Nate saw Sarah watching her, and he saw her take a step toward her, but Mat's wife did not raise her eyes, and Sarah stayed where she was.

145

Mat drained his cup and banged it on the table. "The rest of you git back to your places and git ready to travel. Remember, every family has to go in one wagon."

They began to drift out, but Nathan stayed.

Mat said, "What's the matter with you?"

Nathan took a deep breath. "I'm not satisfied about a lot of things." He sat down across the table from Mat and poured a drink of rye. "I didn't say I wanted to go to Tejas."

"You don't want to stay here and keep up this feud, do you?"

"I'm not sure," said Nathan, "that this *is* my feud."

"They're fightin' the Foleys, ain't they?"

"When I married I figured Sarah became a Price—not me a Foley."

"We've got to hang together," said Mat.

"Nobody has ever told me why."

"Because if they get us divided, they can whip us all separately." Nathan heard a sound, and looked up to see Zer leaning on his cane inside the door. He looked back at Mat. "Nobody ever said they were fighting me."

"You been livin' in smoke, ain't you?"

"Smoke aimed at you—not at me."

"What difference does it make who the bullet's aimed at? You're just as dead when it hits you."

"The difference is," Nathan said slowly, "that if I were living somewhere with just Sarah and my own family, there wouldn't be any feud. I'd get along."

"Ain't you standin' behind the rest of us?"

Nathan said uncomfortably: "It doesn't seem to be a question of standing behind you. The biggest question is: Who gave you the right to deal for me?"

The door opened again, and Sarah slipped in. Nathan

146

glanced at her, and saw Zer watching them attentively.

"You sold my stuff," he said, "and you're telling me what to do with my money."

"What stuff is yours?"

"The crops I've raised, the colts I've foaled, the pigs and calves—"

Mat thundered at him. "All on my land!"

"I never really considered it as being your own land personally."

"It's in my name, isn't it?"

"I suppose so."

"Then the product of my own land belongs to me, doesn't it?"

"I thought you'd say that, but I don't figure it that way," said Nathan, looking straight at him.

"Then who in hell does it belong to?"

"If you put it that way, I'd say it's halvers. You furnished the land, I furnished the work."

Mat's face was turning dark red. "Am I goin' to have mutiny in my own family?"

"This is not mutiny. I want something to say about where I'm going. Sarah is in a family way, and I don't know about takin' her to an uninhabited country. What if we needed a doctor?"

"There's never been a doctor on the place!"

"I know." Nathan looked toward the mountain. "And there are five graves up there. Maybe they wouldn't all be there if you had had a doctor."

There was silence for a moment. Mat's wife, in the corner, was busy carding wool, rolling it into small cylinders that trailed to a point at each end, and stacking them on one another.

Nathan thought she was listening, but he couldn't be sure.

147

He said to Mat: "There's outlaws everywhere down there. They say Little Harpe is around Natchez—and there are others along the Mexican River."

Mat glared at Nathan. "Are you backin' out on me?"

"If you want to put it that way," Nathan said, "I'm thinking about it."

Mat's voice was steely. "If you piker out, don't look for a penny from me."

Nathan's mouth opened, but he closed it. That was to be expected, of course. Mat had always used his property to hold the whip hand over them. If Nathan pulled out now, he would pull out with nothing. He studied Mat. "I had a saddle horse when I came here," he said. "When I pull out, I aim to take the gelding with me."

"What do you aim to do with Sarah?"

Mat knew he was on thin ice there; it was in his eyes if not in his voice.

"Sarah is my wife," Nathan said. "She goes with me."

"What if she doesn't want to?"

Nathan felt a sudden chill. What if Sarah wanted to go with her father? What if her loyalty to her own family was greater than her loyalty to him? He swung in his seat to look at her, and he saw the confusion in her face. He understood the triumph in Mat's eyes when he looked back at him. He took a deep breath and started to speak, but changed his mind. Did he have any right to be so positive before talking to Sarah and finding out what she wanted? On the frontier a wife was supposed to go with her husband, do whatever he said. His word was law. But in reality a wife had considerable influence over what the husband did.

Mat said, "You ready to leave her too?"

Nathan got up and answered stiffly: "Sarah isn't one

148

of your horses or blacks or a bushel of corn. She's my wife, and as such she's entitled to make her own decisions."

Mat grinned again, and it was an evil grin of victory. But Nathan thought there was something else there too—perhaps uncertainty, for was Mat sure of what Sarah would do? Nathan said, "We'd better get home," and Sarah fell in behind him.

Joe was coming back from the oak tree. Nathan and Sarah moved to one side, and Mat met Joe at the door. "Brandon says he'll give us a week."

Being told what he could do and when he could do it must have been a bitter thing for Mat to swallow, but he countered it with defiance, as usual. He glared up at the tree and shook his big fist. "We'll move when we damn' well please!" he shouted. Then, having made this gesture, he turned to Zer. "Better get to work on that road, so the cattle can come through."

"We'll have it cleared in a couple of days," said Zer, looking curiously at Nathan.

Tim visited Nathan after supper. They sat outside while Nathan smoked a cigar. "Hear you was feelin' your oats this afternoon after we left," said Tim.

"I just said some things I thought."

"Would you really give up everything and stay back here?"

Nathan looked at him. "It hasn't come to that yet."

They sat in silence for a while. The ridges were alive with night sounds—an owl hooting, a coon hound baying from somewhere over the mountain, wolves on the north ridge, drifting south with the game. The noises were a good sign, for they meant that no intruders were around the valley that night.

Presently Tim got up and dusted the back of his hunting shirt. "You ain't decided?"

"I'll stick by what I said."

Tim went off in the darkness. He was a good lad, but he had to have somebody tell him what to do. It was a good marriage he had made with Alice, for Alice was inclined to tell others what to do anyway, and her age gave her an advantage over Tim.

Nathan got up and went in. A log was burning slowly in the fireplace, throwing out the kind of warmth a man could bask in, like that of the sun in a protected place on a winter day. He sat there and watched Sarah gritting corn.

Finally she looked up at him and said, "Nate, I think you should have asked me before you talked that way to Mat."

It took him a little by surprise. "A man has to make his own decisions," he said gently.

"But not entirely without consulting his wife."

"I never aimed to do that, but we're being pushed into this trip to the Tejas Country. Mat never asked our opinion in any way, shape, or form."

"Mat's always been that way."

"That doesn't make it right."

"You forget that he's my father."

There was something different about Sarah— something he had never seen there before. Perhaps he had underestimated Mat; Foley might have known what he was talking about.

Nathan said cautiously, "He forgets you are my wife."

"I am his daughter too."

Nathan frowned. "I'm going for a walk," he said.

He looked at her, hoping for some sign of relenting,

but Sarah was strange to him; he never had seen her like this. He went outside and began to climb the hill. He followed the path and came out at the graveyard, just on the edge of the Foley property. He sat there for a while, listening to the night sounds, confused and fearful. He wondered if Sarah would really go with her father, and he had to confess he didn't know.

He went on to the top of the mountain, feeling some relief in physical effort. His walk would give Sarah a chance to think, perhaps to relent a little. He reached the top of the mountain and sat there a while longer, thinking it over. He guessed he had done right in saying what he had to Mat, and he felt better. He got up and went back down.

It was almost midnight when he reached the cabin. He told the dogs to "Git!" and went in. Sarah was still sitting by the fireplace, but he looked into her eyes and saw that she had not changed. "Think better of it, Nate?"

He looked at the fire. She was indeed a daughter of Mat, for she was carrying the fight to the opponent.

"Nothing has changed," he said.

"Nor have I, Nate."

"You married me."

"A wife doesn't become a chattel."

He thought of Mat's wife, but did not speak of her. "A wife goes where her husband goes."

"Not blindly, though, Nate—not blindly."

He had given everything of himself to Sarah, and asked nothing in return but that she do likewise. Now, as he thought of their parting, with her body filled with his child, he knew that he could not endure separation. Their lives were too mingled now. It would be like leaving a part of his own body. Yet that was what she hinted at.

He looked at her, remembering the pleasant days they had spent together, and the passionate nights, and he felt suddenly humble. Though the cost to his pride was great, he walked slowly over to her, put his hand gently on her shining hair, and said, in a low voice, "All right, Sarah, I'll go."

CHAPTER XV

THEY WERE READY ON THE SEVENTH MORNING—EIGHT big wagons filled with food, seed, goods, clothing, sleeping rugs, blankets and quilts. Axes and wooden tubs and leather buckets hung on the sides. Nearly every wife had insisted on certain keepsakes that she would not leave behind. Martha had put in a walnut dining table, and Nancy had included two cribs for the younger ones. Nancy's oldest boy was ten, and growing into another redhaired Mat. Peggy's oldest was twelve, and had the fair face of his mother. Thelma packed her English china into a hogshead with straw; that was one possession, she said, that she would never leave anywhere. Only Mat's wife seemed utterly without feeling of any sort. She exercised no personal choice over what should go into the wagon.

Mat himself was elated, jovial, boisterous—roaring orders as the train got under way. The money—$60,000 in American gold plus over $7,000 Mat had had stashed away, less a thousand for the bulls—was in Mat's wagon, the fourth in line. Mat had them kill a cow and skin it, then pour the coins in a pile on the skin. He brought the corners together and tied them with rawhide. It took Mat and two others to lift the money into the wagon and put it under the seat. They would buy whisky in the Falls, Mat told them—three jugs for each wagon, and a little wine for the women.

Nancy's oldest and Peggy's oldest were detailed to bring up the rear, herding the spare oxen and horses. Each man had a saddle horse; sometimes they would ride; sometimes they would walk; sometimes they

153

would sit in the wagon to drive the four-ox teams.

Nathan watched the bulls straining at the chains, and said to Mat: "They're going downhill now on a pretty good road. What'll it be when we start across the Louisiana country?"

The black stallion was prancing as Mat held it back. "I aim to have six cattle on a team for the pull across to Nacogdoches," he said.

He was a fine figure that morning, his clothes black homespun, his hat black, his mount black. And he rode it like a charger. Nathan could not help feeling a thrill as the leather snappers began to crack and the lead wagon pulled up a slope. They went through the pass where the sides of the valley came almost together, and Nathan, who had gone ahead to be sure the road was clear, sat the bay gelding and watched them pass: Zer's wagon first, then Bert's, then George McGee's, Mat's, his own, Joe's, Ben Metheny's, and Tim's. And Nathan noticed that Mat's wife alone, of all those in the train, failed to turn and look back as they went around the bend that would forever cut them off from Kentucky and the past.

The split hoofs cracked, the oxbows wailed, and the chains gave off reports like pistol shots as the wagons swung down the road. The white canvas billowed in the southwest wind. Nathan waited until the trailing herd had passed. Then he fell in behind, and at the same time he saw Bill Brandon leaning against a tree, a long rifle sticking up through his crossed arms, his face emotionless. As he passed him, Nathan said, "Goodbye, Bill." There was no answer.

The first day out was slow. They crossed the creek and took the turn to the Falls. When they reached higher ground they camped. Mat was in rare good form that night, telling stories of early Kentucky, passing the rye,

154

singing snatches of "Whisky Johnny." With the eight new wagons drawn up in a circle, a big fire in the middle, men smoking or watching the coffee, women busy with clothes and food around the wagons, children running and yelling and playing Indian beyond the wagons, it was a cheerful sight. And yet, Nathan knew, there were many nights to be passed, and they would not all be so cheerful. There were Indians and outlaws and perhaps hostile soldiers to be met before they could get settled in the Tejas Country, and just possibly there might be trouble with the Spanish governor or viceroy or whatever he was. Nathan wasn't too clear on the details of the government, but he had heard many reports of trouble from New Spain. Some got along all right, it was true, and maybe Mat was the one to do it. They would have to find out.

They pulled into the Falls three days later. The oxen were just beginning to get lined out, but they camped on the edge of town while Mat and Zer and Nathan went in to buy flatboats.

For a while they had no luck. Every boat was loaded with goods destined for New Orleans, and none wanted to sell. Then they found a man whose crew had deserted and left him with an Indian bullet wound in his knee. "I'll sell you the boat," he said, "for what it cost me—a dollar a foot. And I can tell you where to get another one like it. You'll need three boats, though, to haul eight wagons and all your stock."

"Three boats?"

"Sure. You don't aim to herd the stock along the bank, do you?"

"That's an idea," said Mat.

"It's no good. You can't make enough time. Anyway, the outlaws would get your stock in no time. Better take my advice and get a third boat for the stock, and get corn to last for a month. That'll take you to Natchez. From there you'll have good grazing. It won't hurt to have your animals corn-fed when you leave Natchez, for there's some hard pulls over to Nacogdoches."

"Do you know anything about getting land in Tejas?" asked Nathan.

"Quite a few are talkin' about it. Understand the gover'ment welcomes the right kind."

"What's the right kind?"

"Mainly them who won't cause no trouble."

Mat asked, "Know where we can get a third boat?"

"Not right now. If I could walk I'd take you down along the river where you ought to be able to pick up one easy. Some fellers come down from Pennsylvania and are satisfied to sell their stuff here. Some go on to New Orleans because they don't want to abandon an expensive boat."

Mat paid for the boat and went to see the second man, who was drinking at a tavern. "Sure, I'll sell at a dollar a foot, and damn' glad to get rid of it. Tired of this river life."

"Seventy-five cents a foot," offered Mat.

"Nope. A dollar—just what I paid."

"Eighty cents."

"You ain't buyin' no rowboat, mister, from no Indian. If it's worth a penny to you, it's worth a dollar."

"All right. Know where I can get a third boat—a smaller one?"

The man looked at him. "Sure, I do. See Ed Hunt in the back room."

Mat bought the third boat from Hunt, who asked where they were going.

"To New Spain," said Mat.

156

"Down to Natchez, eh? Got a patroon?"

"A what?"

"A pilot."

"Don't see no need for one. The river goes where she goes."

"That's where you're fooled, mister. The Ohio is full of rapids, especially around the Cave-in-Rock country, and there's a hundred mile there where you got to know the river to get a boat through this time of year."

"These boats don't draw over two or three feet of water, do they?"

"That's right—but the water's low this time of year. Take my advice and hire a patroon, mister. Sixty dollars a month and cheap at half the price."

"I heard about the rapids," said Zer. "One boat lost would pay for a patroon for a long time."

"Maybe we could use him down to the Mississippi," said Mat.

"Don't fool yourself, mister. The Mississippi is ten times worse."

"How worse?"

"The Mississippi is full of snags and sawyers and floating islands and real islands. You never know which way to go, and you can lose three, four days in a backwater. Then there's a whopping big swamp t'other side."

"How big?"

"Fifty, sixty mile wide and near fifteen hundred mile long."

"Fifteen hundred!" said Zer.

"Smack dab to the Gulf of Mexico."

"We don't aim to navigate no swamps."

"That there's the trouble. There's so many channels in the river a man never knows, and sometimes the

157

strongest channel leads into this here swamp, and the first thing you know you're down in this swamp and you can stay there till the spring floods."

"You mean the river is higher than the land?"

"Sounds crazy, mister, but that's the gospel truth. The banks of the river have built up higher than the land, and when the river overflows it makes channels into the swamp. Then the river goes down and everything's all right, but some night she comes up on you and you won't even know it, and she overflows into the swamp, and you might foller it if you don't know."

"Sounds like you're tryin' to scare us up, mister."

"Give me no attention, then. Pay me for the boat and take it on your own. But I'll tell you one thing: that Mississippi is the damnedest river *you* ever seen!"

They talked it over. Mat, for once, wasn't quite as headstrong as usual. They went up and down, talking to boatmen, finding a couple who had been all the way down, and who shook their heads at the idea of a man navigating the Mississippi without knowing it. "Better get a patroon, mister," they advised. "It's only a month to Natchez-or less. Cost you $50 or so."

They set out to find a pilot. They found one who would take them to New Madrid, the first Spanish town they would encounter, and there, the man told them, they could find a man to finish the trip, for New Madrid was a river town, and its inhabitants were as much rivermen as the people of Dover were fishermen.

They examined the boats, which looked sound enough; but Mat pointed out that they were filthy. "We'll get the women to scrubbing them up," he said.

Mat's wife took charge of one. With the help of Peggy, she had it clean in a couple of days, except for a pile of old cowhides that Nathan threw in the river.

They kept the horses and a few chickens and small pigs in the first two boats, and prepared room for the oxen in the last boat. Then Katherine found they didn't have a milch cow, and insisted they could not take the children into a strange country without a cow. Mat, to quiet her, bought two cows and put them in the second boat.

The man who had sold them the third boat shook his head when the boats tipped as they drove aboard. "You better leave about three-quarters of that stuff here," he said. "You'll be throwing it out along the way anyway."

"I am not leaving my walnut table," Martha said. "That was my mother's, and it's the only thing left that is my own."

"I'm not giving up my English china," Thelma said. "That was my great-great-aunt's, and it goes where I go."

The old man looked at them both. "The time could come, missus, when you would change your mind about that."

"We've got plenty of oxen," said the red-haired Peggy.

"Oxen play out, ma'am. Sometimes they die, and sometimes the Indians get 'em."

"Surely," said Katherine, "there is law in Louisiana."

"Yes, ma'am, there's law anywhere—but sometimes you have to make it yourself."

"Are there really wild Indians down there?" asked Katherine's oldest boy.

"They're sure as wild as the Shawnees and Delawares ever were."

"What kinds?"

"Mighty nigh every kind—Comanches, Lipans, man-eatin' Karankawas, Caddoes, Osage, Arkansa. But I reckon the worst of all is the outlaw Choctaws."

"What's that?"

"Indians that got chased out of the Choctaw Nation by their own tribe. Them is bad Indians."

"Yip-pee!"

"I ain't just talkin'," the old man said to Mat. "It'll take plenty of guts to herd this outfit where you're goin'."

"It took plenty to come to Kentucky," Mat reminded.

The old man nodded. "Your funeral. Best take three rifles apiece. Then the women can load while the men shoot—case of Indians."

They got four wagons on a boat and disposed of the stock. They used the canvas from the wagons to make lean-tos for shade for the women and children. By then it was noon.

"Don't try to graze your stock until you leave the Ohio," they were told.

"Why?" asked Mat.

"Outlaws. They're thick as thieves from Red Banks down to Smithland. But old Josh, your patroon, knows all that. He'll see you get to New Madrid if you follow his advice."

"I've done some boating on the Susquehanna," said Mat stiffly.

"It don't count up until you've been down the Mississippi—and you'll see why, mister. She's big as an ocean and changeable as a woman. She'll rise overnight this time of year, even, or she'll fall and leave you on a sandbar you never knew was there." He shook his head. "Don't fool with the river, mister. Maybe the Spaniards you can out-talk and the Injuns you can outfight, but the river is bigger than any man that ever lived."

Nathan thought that perhaps Mat was impressed, but Mat, as usual, tried to hide it.

160

"I ain't sayin' it can't be done," the man said. "I'm sayin' to keep your eye peeled."

"We'll do that," Mat said impatiently.

Zer said: "It's dinnertime. Reckon we better go to a tavern?"

Mat roared: "Hell, no! It'd cost a fortune to feed this bunch at a tavern. We'll cook on board."

Nathan glanced at Zer, and his opinion of Zer dropped, for Zer looked at his fingers and then away. It was obvious that it would take several hours to prepare a meal, and the kids would be fussy and everybody would be yelling at one another; but Zer didn't speak up, and so Nathan did.

"I think you'd better feed 'em here. Save a lot of trouble."

Mat's eyes narrowed. "Am I goin' to have trouble with you, Nate?"

"You may," said Nathan.

Mat glared at him. "We'll eat on board!" he shouted. "Everybody on board!"

The pilot stood in the bow of the leading boat, his hands on the sweep oar. Mat stood beside him, legs widespread, facing downriver, a splendid figure in his black clothes. Nathan had stayed back to handle the ropes that held the boats. He untied one and threw it into the water. The pilot began to work the sweep. Then Alice's penetrating voice rose above the lapping of water and the creaking of wet wood. "Ma! Ma's left behind!"

Mat turned at the hips, looking back at the bank. A quirk of annoyance moved the corners of his mouth. He shouted at her, "Get aboard, Ma!"

But Mat's wife did not move. Small and lonely she looked, in her drab homespun dress and her calico sundown. The sundown, Nathan realized suddenly, was the only article of dress-up she ever wore.

Mat ran back along the boat, dodging around the wagons and the lean-tos. "What's the matter with you?" he cried.

She didn't answer him, but just stood there. Nathan came up. "I'll help you, Mrs. Foley."

Her tired old eyes turned on him. There was gratefulness in her wrinkled face, but she said, "I don't need any help, Nate."

"Get on the second boat!" roared Mat.

She stood, shaking her head. It was incredible that so small and helpless a creature should defy a magnificent man like Mat Foley, but she shook her head, and there was something about her that made Nathan know she would not change her decision.

Mat leaped off the back end of the boat. "What in hell's the matter with you?"

She looked up at him. "I'm not going with you, Mat."

His face was like a thundercloud. "What do you want me to do—beg you?"

"I don't want anything, Mat. I brought you nothing and I take nothing away. But I'm not going to New Spain."

"Why didn't you tell me this before?"

"You never asked me."

Mat was more furious than Nathan ever had seen him. "Do you want to give up everything?"

Her voice was clear. "I'm not giving up anything, Mat. I never had anything. You made all the decisions. You bought everything. I never had a piece of money in my hands in my life."

Nathan was stunned.

Mat couldn't believe her defiance, and Nathan knew

what Mat was thinking—not that here was a woman who had come to the end of her endurance, but that here was a woman who was making a fool of him. He said, "You're crazy, woman!"

"Maybe I am, Mat, but I'm not going to New Spain with you." Mat frowned. It was a situation that baffled him. "What'll you do? How will you make a living?"

She looked at her hands, gnarled and worn. "The same as I always have," she said. "Scrubbing and cooking."

Mat swore.

"I've got kin buried back on that mountain," she said. "Two children of my own, two grandchildren, and your own sister that needed someone to love her—but you brought her back here to lord it over her with your money and your ways, Mat Foley. You killed her as sure as you killed the Brandon boy."

"She was sick. She would have died anyway."

"Your way was quicker," said Mat's wife.

"Cast off !" called the pilot.

Nathan ran to unwind the rope. He had a glimpse of Mat's face as he went by. Mat was trying to decide how to make her pay for the indignity she had put upon him. Suddenly Mat turned and jumped back on board the boat. Nathan threw the line into the water, and the bow, already caught by the current, began to edge the boat along while the pilot worked the sweep.

Mat did not look back. Nathan watched until the boat was out in the current, then he ran to unwind the lines on the second boat, piloted by Bert Foley.

It too edged into the stream. And still the woman stood there. Nobody raised a hand to wave goodbye, and she watched them, dry-eyed, inscrutable. Perhaps, thought Nathan, there were no tears left in her.

He went to cast off the third boat, piloted by Zer. He loosed the bow rope, and Zer began to work the sweep. Mat's wife was still standing there, little and old and tired but very sure of herself. Nathan reached inside the wallet formed by the lap-over of his hunting shirt. Pulling out a package of cigars, and two gold coins wrapped in a piece of buckskin, he ran to Mat's wife, pressed the coins into her work-worn hands, whispered, "Good fortune!" and ran back to the stern rope. He cast it off quickly and jumped on board, then turned.

Mat's wife had not moved, but her face was raised.

Sarah met him with tears. "What happened between Mother and Mat?"

"Your mother," he told her, "made up her own mind."

CHAPTER XVI

NO WORD WAS EVER SAID TO MAT, OR ASKED OF HIM, about Ma, either as wife or as mother. At one moment she was with them; in the next moment she was behind, in another world, under Mat's disfavor; and few seemed to dare to wonder whether she would eat or starve. Only Sarah had a haunted look in her eyes as she sometimes faced back upriver.

They drifted down, Mat spelling the patroon at the first boat, Bert and George taking turns on the second boat and getting the feel of it, and Tim and Nathan spelling Zer on the third boat.

The Ohio was broad and majestic; it ran through deep valleys and among hills covered with maple and black walnut trees, with occasionally a great sycamore raising its white branches like ghostly arms over them all.

In a few days they negotiated the Grand Chain of Rocks, and shortly after moored at New Madrid, a town with streets a hundred feet wide and a park in the center. Here Spanish soldiers in black and white swallowtail coats still walked guard, although the Americans were moving in. Here they discharged their pilot and took on a new man who said he had been down the "big creek" eleven times and knew every rock and tree in it. "And ye'd best know them, too, if ye want to get where you're going."

"How much to Natchez?"

"Not so much. You're takin' off for Spanish country?"

"Yes."

"Lots of 'em are. People are sayin' it will be part of

165

the United States before long."

Mat ignored that. "How much?"

"Natchez? About 200 leagues—600 miles. If nothing happens we'll make sixty miles a day—about ten days. Say $30 for the trip."

"When can you leave?"

"Couple of days. Any hurry?"

"We want to get where we're goin'," said Mat.

"We'll raise Natchez, don't worry."

"How about passports?"

"You better see Henri Peyroux. He's commandant of the post."

"Sounds like a Frenchman."

"You'll find all kinds in the service of Spain—plenty of Irish, like yourself."

"Irish?"

"Why not? Alejandro O'Reilly was captain-general at Havana not too many years ago."

"They must like it."

"Most of 'em get where they can get some extra piasters by keeping their eyes open. It's good pay, that way."

"You mean bribery?" asked Mat.

The man shrugged. "Call it what you want. It's an easy way to get along—for everybody."

"You mean to say the officials know it?"

"All the way up and down the line, mister. You want something in Spain, and you have trouble gettin' anywhere, try a gold piece. Course, be careful. You can't get to the higher-ups so easy."

It seemed obvious, thought Nathan, that Mat was getting his first lesson in Spanish politics. Mat might bristle at the suggestion of paying a bribe, but he was pleased at the power of his money.

"Better take all your menfolks with you when you see Peyroux. He'll want to look 'em over."

Under guidance of their patroon, whose name was Hersh, they saw the French commandant the next morning. He was very courteous and asked their business through an interpreter. Mat said they were going for settlement, and he seemed pleased. "It is fortunate that you have stop' here for passports. It is an indication that you intend no breaking of the law."

"We've always gone by the law," said Mat.

The commandant drew a large sheet of paper toward him. "I will give you a pass for yourself, three sons and their wives, four daughters and their husbands. There is no wife of yours?"

Mat said harshly, "No."

"Very well, m'sieur. This will take you to Nacogdoches. I would advise you to proceed promptly, for Louisiana has now been sold to the United States, and we do not know when it will become a possession of your country. In such a case, is hardly necessary to point out that your passport will be of no value."

He wrote down the names of all the adults. "The children do not matter. There will be more or fewer of them by the time you reach Nacogdoches."

"Can I get my land in Béjar?"

"I do not know that, m'sieur. Louisiana is under Havana, while Tejas is under the viceroy in Méjico. The best I can tell you is to inquire at Nacogdoches."

"All right."

"A word about your character, m'sieur. Do you perhaps know someone in New Madrid?"

"I don't know anybody, but"—Mat's chest swelled—"I've got $66,000 in gold in my wagons."

"That is a fair recommendation, I am sure, though we

167

had a man named Mason here not long ago, with several sons, who had $7,000 in Spanish piasters but who has turned out to be a thorough pirate."

"I'm not—"

Peyroux smiled. "I have examine' your boats, m'sieur. With such a cargo I am sure you intend what you say." He signed the paper "Henri Peyroux," and gave it to Mat. "I advise you to keep very quiet about the money you have in your wagons. M'sieur Mason, the pirate, is at large in the vicinity of Natchez."

"And he's the one—"

"We sent him to New Orleans for trial, but he escaped."

"We'll take care of ourselves," said Mat.

"My very best wishes, m'sieur."

They left New Madrid two days later. The reason for the delay Nathan never learned, except that Hersh was not ready to go, and kept speaking of the "rise" in the water. Nathan kept an eye on Hersh after that.

Samuel Mason, vainly trying to cover his projecting tooth with his upper lip, looked coldly at Woman Claydon and said: "Get on the gray and ride across Louisiana to the Sabine. Find that damn' Frenchman, Krudenier. Tell him what I said: there's a train of wagons'll be at the Sabine in a couple of weeks. They're only two days from Natchez right now."

Claydon considered. "How many wagons?"

"Eight wagons. An old man and seven sons and daughters, all married."

"Krudenier doesn't know me," said Claydon.

"Tell him this old man had a big plantation in Kentucky, but he got in trouble with his neighbors and they run him out. They all sold their places." Mason rose, his wolfish tooth projecting. "That's why they're carryin' so much gold—$66,000."

"Will Krudenier know what to do?"

Mason said sourly, "Krudenier always knows what to do." Claydon nodded, his high, shining forehead glistening in the sun.

"And you stay there and collect my share."

Claydon's small black eyes became sharper than usual. "You mean from Krudenier?"

Mason said, "Him and me has an arrangement for things like this."

Claydon said slowly: "He may not want to give me a part of the gold. He's boss of the Twilight Zone, isn't he?"

"What you think I'm sendin' *you* for? If you act like you expect to get it, he'll give it to you."

Claydon said flatly, "I'll expect to get it."

Mason seemed satisfied. "When you say it like that, he'll give it to you. Now there's only one thing to remember. You won't have too much trouble getting to Krudenier if you're careful. After you leave Avoyelles you better watch sharp, because them cutthroats in the zone'd kill you for your horse." He grinned. "You get to the ferry on the Sabine. Krudenier has a place somewhere around there."

"I'll find him."

"That's the easy part," Mason reminded him. "The hard part will come when you put that gold on your horse and start back here. He won't like you bringing back all that money—and neither will his men."

Claydon thought it over, keeping his eyes on Mason's but not really seeing them. "If I get to Krudenier," he said, "then I've got to get away from him alive and come back through three hundred miles of killers." His

169

black eyes glittered. "How much are you payin' me for this trip?"

Mason said coldly, "I figured you'd ask that. All you're interested in is your percentage."

"Nothin' wrong with that."

Mason's flat stare was on him. "Some day it'll pay you to wonder what the other man's thinkin', instead of just how much are you goin' to get."

"I'll look out for that," Claydon said.

Mason watched him. "You get one-fourth of what you bring back."

It was more than Claydon had expected. But he looked toward a curl of smoke coming up from a clearing beyond the canebrake. He listened to the voices. Then he looked back. "We captured a woman in that pack train this morning. A Spanish officer's wife. We drew lots for her." He looked back at the smoke and moistened his lips. "I drew fourth," he said pleadingly.

Mason answered: "There'll be more women tomorrow and next day and next day. Whenever there's men, there's women—but ain't every day there's a chance at this much money." He threw the reins to Claydon, and Claydon saw that Mason knew what torture he was going through. But Mason said, "Get started—and bring back every sou of my share."

Claydon took a deep breath. He looked at the smoke and then mounted the horse. His two hundred and forty pounds made the gray gather its haunches. Claydon settled himself in the saddle. "*If* I get back," he said.

Mason's answer was acidulous. "You sure as hell don't look like no fighter. You're too fat in the face and you look punchy around the stomach. Your feet are too slim and your face is too narrow. You've got eyes like a snake, that tell everybody what you're going to do. But you're strong as a bull on the prod and you're quick as a water moccasin and you're tricky as a Mississippi tiger. Next to me and John Setton—blast his dirty soul—you're the killin'est man in Mississippi Territory, because you like killin' better than anything but women. You'll come back if you want to—and you better want to."

Claydon looked at the smoke coming up from beyond the canebrake. His black eyes glittered in his pale face. Then Mason slogged the gray in the belly with his knee, and the horse bolted down the trail to Natchez.

After a while, when the fever had somewhat subsided in his brain, Claydon remembered the various caches of gold he had made along the Trace northeast of Natchez. All told, they made a considerable sum, and maybe it was time for him to collect them and move out of the country, to Mexico, to Acapulco. One fact deterred him: both Mason and Harpe were still alive, and it might be that Harpe was suspicious, for there were times when he seemed too stupid. It was possible that Mason was trying to push him, Claydon, into revealing his caches; Mason had done things like that before. So Claydon resolutely set his face ahead and kept the gray going toward Natchez. He wasn't going to be caught in any trap like that.

Two hours later, by the time he had ridden the slow ferry across the mile-wide Mississippi and by-passed the small settlement of Concordia and the fort, Claydon was beginning to get himself under control. He hadn't forgotten the Spanish woman, but he was able to think a little, and he began to figure up the odds.

Mason had promised him a fourth, but Mason wasn't doing any of the work. Mason had sent other men across to the Sabine with messages for Krudenier—and some of them hadn't come back. They were supposed to have

171

been killed, but Claydon wondered.

Where was Bloody Harpe? Had he gone to the Sabine for Mason, and, if he had gotten the money, had he kept going? Was that why Mason had cursed him? Claydon wondered as he rode along. What was to keep him from having the whole thing? It would be a lot more than he had hidden along the Trace and it would take him anywhere he wanted to go—Mexico City, Havana, Santo Domingo. There were women in those places—women of all colors. Claydon moistened his lips.

He rode across the ridge. At first the willows were saplings; then they grew taller by steps, so that he could tell each year's growth from the next. Then the land went down into swamp, and he followed a zigzag trail for miles. Finally he got into the wooded uplands, into scattered groves of ash, gum, and dogwood. It was October, and the dogwood fruit was ripening into dashes of bright scarlet. He turned southwest. That evening he shot a deer and ate a hindquarter, half cooked, half raw; it might be days before he would dare to fire his rifle again.

He reached the Black River and went down into the blackdirt swamps. It was a sunny day, and alligators lay like logs on the mud banks, almost submerged among the cypress and palmettos. That night he bore out Mason's evaluation of him as a killing man by knocking over a pelican with a stick, although few men could get within gunshot of the big birds. It tasted fishy, but it was food.

He swam the Red River on the gray and went on to Avoyelles. The settlement was located on a large island of prairie, with all the houses facing outward. Claydon made a wide circle around the town and the fort, to avoid officials who might be looking for him, to avoid

Krudenier's spies, and also to avoid any trap that Mason might have laid for him. Up near Walnut Hills, for instance, where Claydon had found the jewels—Mason and even Harpe had asked a lot of questions about that pack train.

Claydon finished the dried meat in his saddlebag, and found some hardtack in a wrecked immigrant wagon. He went on up the Red toward the prairie country. He skirted Rapides. The river was not as wide up there, but the banks were bold and steep, indicating depth.

On the fifth afternoon he cut south to avoid Natchitoches, and made a dry camp in a persimmon grove on a piece of high ground. He studied his back trail; then he looked west. A spiral of smoke came up from beyond Natchitoches, and Claydon knew it meant either Indians or freebooters, for only they would burn a wagon. He was in the Twilight Zone itself now, and somewhere in this nest of outlawry and murder was the man to whom he had to deliver Mason's message.

He did not build a fire that night. Coffee could wait. He sat with his back against the scaly bark of a persimmon tree and let the gray feed in the grass away from the grove while he held the end of a rawhide stake rope and his little black eyes watched the smoke curling up from the northwest. It rose in three distinct columns before it thinned and blended.

He sat cross-legged, with a long Mills muzzle-loader across his legs, a single-shot pistol in the waist of his brown Holland cloth pants, and a long-bladed knife in his right boot, the guard resting in a rawhide loop. He chewed slowly on the last of his hardtack, and then, when it was almost dark, put a load of snuff in his lower lip and sat for a while as the gray snipped off the grass with a crunching sound that annoyed him because he had eaten only hardtack. He jerked impatiently on the rawhide rope. The horse's head came up. It tried to reach the grass again, but Claydon whipped a loop along the rope that jerked its head to one side.

Claydon stood up. He wore an old blue army campaign hat that he had taken from one of Wilkinson's officers who had had the poor judgment to travel the Trace alone, and a buckskin shirt, laced at the throat. A powderhorn swung over one shoulder, and a cartouche bag or bullet pouch and tobacco container over the other; a small sack of salt was in with the tobacco. His face, beginning to lose its fat now, was covered with a week's growth of light brown whiskers.

He shook a persimmon tree half a dozen times, and the ripe yellow fruit came plopping down on the dead leaves around him. He picked up a hatful—the first dozen always tasted good—and pulled the gray into the deeper brush of the grove. He tied the rope around the gray's head so that it would shut off its own wind if it opened its mouth to whinny, and then crawled into a patch of wild grapevine, keeping low to avoid breaking the heavy spiderweb, and beating the ground before him with the end of the rope to run off snakes. When he got in the middle of a thicket of wild sweet-potato vines, he covered his head with the horse blanket to keep off the gnats, and went to sleep.

CHAPTER XVII

THE THREE FLATBOATS OF THE FOLEYS FLOATED downriver, past Little Prairie, past limestone bluffs. On the left, as they rode the brown water, the bank grew higher and steeper. On the right was the seemingly limitless swamp. The cane grew bigger and bigger, and below the Arkansas River they began to see cypress and moss, but no more wild turkeys. Wolves howled nightly on the east side of the river but not on the west. Alligators were seen after they passed Chickasaw Bluffs. Indians sometimes came down to the edge of the water, looked over the three boats traveling together, and went away. Others came alongside in canoes and wanted to buy tobacco or whisky, trading deer meat, bear meat, and sometimes buffalo.

The wisdom of engaging a pilot was soon evident, for in places the river had many currents, and it was a world of islands and trees and matted wood, with brown water everywhere, flowing in all directions. There were tricks, too, in knowing where to camp at night, for there were always falling banks, and islands caving away under the corrosive action of the tremendous waters.

Occasionally, when they could find an open place in the forests or the canebrake, they would pull in to the shore and let the animals out to graze for a couple of hours and stretch their limbs. But they watched closely, and all the men carried loaded rifles whenever they were on shore.

Their first encounter with white men came on their last day above Natchez. They had started before sunup that morning, anticipating a long run to make Natchez

175

by sundown, but as the sun rose above the canebrake a skiff put out from the east shore and came to meet them. The three boats were riding abreast at that time, with Mat's boat in the middle, and Nathan heard all that was said.

There were five men in the skiff, and they waited for the three flatboats to catch up with them.

Mat, standing in the bow of the center boat, said to the pilot, "I don't like the looks of that load."

"They're probably travelers," said Hersh, "who have fallen into trouble."

"What kind of trouble?" Mat growled.

"They may have been put upon by outlaws, their wagons burned—"

"Wagons?" thundered Mat. "No wagon can travel the Natchez Trace. It isn't wide enough. Any fool knows that."

The pilot hesitated, and Nathan watched him. "Well, there's lots of ways to get in trouble in the wilderness."

"Ahoy!" Mat shouted through his hands. "What do you want?"

A scowling-faced man with a low forehead answered. "We were set upon by Indians and they took our rifles."

"What kind of Indians?"

"Choctaws."

The flatboats were about to overtake the skiff, which two men kept in place by slow handling of the oars.

The pilot said aside to Mat, "Want to let them come aboard?"

Nathan listened for the answer. Mat said: "Absolutely not. Maybe they're outlaws."

"Not on this part of the river."

"On *any* part of the river, according to what they said at the Falls."

Hersh looked disgruntled and turned back to his work. The skiff came into the space between the two flatboats, and was now only forty feet or so from Nathan. He didn't like the looks of the men. They were hard men—hard-eyed, hard-faced—and it was not the kind of hardness that came from the weather, but that which came from inside. Nathan turned his head to look into Sarah's eyes at his shoulder. "Get my rifle," he whispered.

Her eyes widened. A moment later he felt the barrel under his fingers.

The men in the skiff were still arguing with Mat. "All we want is a little flour and some rifles."

"What would you use to pay for it?"

"We have money," said one, holding up a handful of round coins that glistened dully in the sun.

"How come," said Mat, "the Choctaws didn't take your money?"

"We had it hid."

"Don't sound good to me," said Mat. "Anyway, we got no extra rifles or ammunition. We need all we've got."

The skiff was now floating alongside the flatboat, and two men reached out and grasped the side of the flatboat. Nathan brought up his rifle. "Take your hands away from that boat," he said across the water.

The leader, the one who was doing the talking, turned quickly to look at Nathan. He said something under his breath, and the two men took their hands away from the flatboat.

"Now git the hell away from here," Mat roared, "before we open up on you. You're a bunch of damned pirates and you know it!"

"We was just lookin' for help."

177

"Every one of you is fat and sassy. You ain't been in no trouble. Now git, and remember—there's rifles on you from all sides." Mat was quite a magnificent figure when things were going his way.

Nathan lowered his rifle slowly, and looked at the pilot from New Madrid. It might have been Nathan's imagination, but he thought the man was displeased.

In half an hour the skiff was out of sight, having drawn back to the eastern shore. The three big boats were still abreast, and Nathan went up to spell Zer at the sweep oar.

Zer asked, "Did you really think them fellers were outlaws?"

Nathan almost felt contempt as he answered, "Didn't you?"

Zer frowned. "They said they was in trouble."

So that was what came from living under Mat's thumb for thirty-five years. When the crisis had arisen over Pete Brandon, Zer had opposed Mat because he was on familiar ground, but now abruptly he was thrown into a new environment, in unfamiliar surroundings, and he was helpless, with neither the experience to judge nor the firmness to decide. What would such a man, sheltered in the State of Foley all his life, do when he found himself in Tejas, surrounded by hostility on every side? Nathan felt himself suddenly mature. He had had some admiration for Zer, but now . . . Nathan shook his head. All any man needed was one good look at that bunch of ruffians to know they were not travelers as they claimed.

As he thought back on it, the one who had done the talking seemed familiar to him. He prodded his memory but could not bring anything into the open. A heavy, scowling-faced man, of less than average height, with curly hair that came low over his forehead: somewhere he had seen or heard of a man like that, but right now he couldn't remember where.

Nathan looked at Zer and said pointedly, "They could *say* they were pelicans."

Zer turned back without a word.

They pulled up at Natchez-Under-the-Hill that evening. Mat and Zer and Bert went on shore to arrange for sale of the boats and to buy some peach brandy. The shelf under the high hill was a scene of constant activity that night, along with boisterous and obscene talk, drunkenness, and sharp-eyed girls.

Sarah looked on disapprovingly, and Nathan sat with his shoulder against hers, watching, while the oxen crunched corn in the middle of the boat.

All of the men returned from the Gallo Negro after midnight, and Mat said they would get $15 apiece for the boats, to be broken up and used for lumber. He had bought three two-gallon kegs of peach brandy at two shillings a pint, and some heavy planks. He had also hired a guide.

Zer gave Nathan a small piece of heavy paper, saying, "I reckon you was right about the pirates."

Nathan read the printed circular slowly by the light of a candle. "Proclamation. A certain Samuel Mason and one Wiley Harpe from Kentucky and their gang have made headquarters near the Walnut Hills and have boarded boats and killed the owners. These sons of rapine and murder must be stopped. A reward of $400 is offered by the Secretary of War, and $500 by myself as governor. W. C. C. Claiborne, Governor of Mississippi Territory."

Nathan stared at the paper, seeing again the scowling, stocky man on the boat. "That's it!" He turned, but Zer had lain down under a tarpaulin and was already asleep.

"What is it?" asked Sarah at Nathan's shoulder.

"Uh—" He looked at her in the candlelight. Sarah had her own problems; this was one he could handle himself. "I was going to say something to Zer," he said. "It wasn't important."

He dropped the circular over the side into the brown water. The man in the boat had been Bloody Harpe.

The revelry on the shelf continued all night, and the next morning it was almost deserted as the Foleys poled their three boats back into the main stream and worked them over to the other side. The current pulled them down about two miles, but they found a good place to land. They tied the boats to willow trees and prepared a runway for the wagons, using the planks.

By mid-morning the wagons were rumbling off onto land. The pilot, Hersh, was paid off and left in charge of the boats. Then the bulls put their shoulders into the yokes and the train moved out and up toward Fort Concordia. Mat waved them on while he himself stopped to have the passports checked. He rode back exuberant. "He says the Spanish gover'ment is glad to see us! They want men who know the soil!"

"I hope he's speaking for the viceroy in Mexico," said Nathan. Mat glanced at him and rode on. He was having his way, and though it looked like a triumph Nathan did not like it. On every hand were evidences of deception, treachery, and outlawry, with no commitment by anyone in authority as to what lay ahead. He was very sober as they camped that night.

It was sixteen days to Natchitoches. The character of the country changed. They left the eternal swamps behind.

180

Starwort and coral plant began to appear on the high land, and around the bayous were great banks of Carolina jessamine with a fragrant yellow flower. Here they saw their first mistletoe, a dark green plant that grew on trees. Violets appeared in shady places, and buttercups in open meadows. Kingfishers, sandpipers, pelicans, and cedar birds were seen and identified. Here was excellent grass, and the oxen had little need for corn after three weeks of inactivity. They pulled strongly, and only occasionally was it necessary to hook an extra pair to a wagon to get it up a steep hill or through a soft spot.

At night they put the wagons into a circle around a big fire. The animals grazed under guard, and Mat told them about early days in Kentucky. He had followed Boone, he said, by a very few years, and had worked at Boone's Lick for a while when the Pottawatomies were looking for hair. Then he had found the valley and had determined it should be his. In the same way, he said, they would establish their empire in Tejas.

Sarah was getting quite large, and Nathan tried to make an easy place for her to sit in the wagon by piling up bearskins in back of the seat. One night she said to him, "You don't like this trip, do you, Nate?"

He shook his head.

"Don't you see his enthusiasm? Don't you feel his tremendous vitality? He's doing something most men would be afraid to do.

"He is doing it with other people," Nathan said stubbornly. "He is risking the lives of fourteen grownups and nineteen children, with two more on the way." (for Katherine was obviously pregnant too).

"You can't help but admire his aggressiveness. He never loses sight of what he wants to do."

181

He looked at the bright light in her eyes—the light that was Mat himself. "But that's not the whole story," he said. "No one else has had a chance to say what they want to do."

"It still isn't too late."

"I'm thinking of that," he said, and saw the sudden alertness flash over her face.

"Don't you think Mat can do it?"

"Mat can't fight for all of us. Each man has to protect his own family."

"From what?"

He said gently: "Sarah, you are failing to see a lot of things. You never saw anything except what went on in your valley, did you?"

"Sometimes we went to a housewarming. That's how I met you."

Nathan was uncomfortable. "I've made my own way since I can remember," he said. "And this trip doesn't look good to me. The country here is different. Kentucky is settled. The Indians are no longer a problem there. Outlaw gangs have been broken up. But this land is bigger than anything we know. It's more hostile. It's the wilderness all over again—under a strange government that gives us no assurance of anything."

"Don't you think Mat knows what he's doing?"

"No."

She was silent a long time. Then, "What are you going to do?"

"You may as well be prepared. Within two nights we shall reach Natchitoches." He took a deep breath. "At Natchitoches you and I are leaving the train."

"Nate!"

"You and our baby are my responsibility," he went

182

on. "I would not be a man if I did not take care of you to the best of my conscience."

"Mat will never allow it."

"It is not Mat's decision," he said.

When they pulled into the outskirts of Natchitoches, the jumping-off place for the Tejas Country, all the men went with Mat to report to the commandant. He looked them over and said: "All good, strong men. You have arms?"

"Yes.

"The Twilight Zone, which you will enter after leaving Natchitoches, is dangerous. There are many armed gangs of bandits."

"Doesn't the gover'ment furnish protection?" asked Mat.

"There are soldiers—but unfortunately both Louisiana and Tejas are huge areas. We try to protect the helpless, but I think you must know that the final protection will come from yourselves."

Mat said: "We can handle any situation that comes up. We have your permission to go on?"

"You do. And *buena suerte, señor*—good luck."

They went back to the train. The women had supper ready—ash cake, fried ham, and deer stew. After supper Mat broke out a keg of peach brandy and passed it around the fire. "To Tejas!" he shouted, holding his cup high.

Sarah looked at Nathan. Nathan looked at Mat. "I have something to say to you." His voice was clear and firm, and some of the men around the fire looked up. "I will drink to Tejas," said Nathan, "because you are going there. But I and my family are not going to be with you." He emptied the tin cup. "To Tejas!"

Mat stared at him. At first he was astounded. Then he was indignant. Finally his black eyes became pin points of fury, and he said, "What the hell are you talkin' about?"

"Sarah and I are staying here at Natchitoches."

"You backing out?"

"You may call it that," said Nathan. "I call it using good sense."

"Good sense!" roared Mat.

"Every place we have turned we have run into outlaws and treachery. Our pilot coming down the Mississippi tried to sell us out to the five men in the skiff."

"You're out of your mind!"

"Not altogether. That was Bloody Harpe—Little Harpe, they used to call him in Kentucky—in that boat, and Hersh tried to get you to take them aboard. That was on the open Mississippi, supposedly in protected waters, only one day from Natchez. What will it be like west of Natchitoches, where even the commandant admits there is no law?"

"We've got our rifles."

"We also have women and children. We have no fort, nothing but wagons. And a wagon does not stop a bullet."

"Who is going to shoot at us?"

"Anybody who knows you have a cowhide full of gold in your wagon."

"How can anybody know that?"

"You announced it to the commandant at New Madrid, before the ears of our flatboat pilot."

"He wouldn't—"

"He *did!*" Nathan insisted. "He tried to get you to let those five men aboard. They would have bought rifles

184

and turned them on you."

"I wouldn't have sold."

"Two men had their hands on the flatboat," Nathan pointed out. "They pulled back only when they saw my rifle aimed at them."

"And because of that you think—"

"That is only one thing. There are many things. But talk is idle. I merely say to you that I wish you good fortune in the Tejas Country."

Mat choked for an instant. His face was black. "If you drop out here, you'll go without a cent."

"I expected that," said Nathan.

"You held out some money of your own, then!"

"No, I haven't a cent."

Mat's face in the red glow of the fire was a study in amazement, in bafflement, in indignation. "I suppose you've talked up this mutiny to the whole train."

"Ask them and find out for yourself."

Mat glared around the fire at the circle of blank faces. For a moment Nathan thought George McGee was about to perjure himself, but George saw Nathan's eyes on him and apparently decided to keep still. Mat looked back at Nathan.

"By God!" he thundered. "Are you deciding for my daughter too?"

Nathan looked at him calmly. "Did you decide for your wife?" He looked around at the seven men. "She had more guts than the lot of you!"

"Maybe Sarah will have something to say about it."

"It may be."

"*Sary!*"

She came into the light. "Yes, Mat."

"Do you know what this—this husband of yours wants to do?" Her frightened eyes found Nathan's. "He

185

told me about it two days ago."

"What are *you* aimin' to do?" Mat demanded.

Her mouth opened. She looked at Nathan and closed it. Her golden hair was shimmering in the firelight.

Mat said, "I'll cut you off without a cent."

Still she looked at Nathan, and he smiled softly. She looked back at her father.

"He hasn't got a cent," Mat said. "He admitted it."

A curious change came over her then. She looked at Nathan, and her eyes seemed to glow. She looked back at Mat. "He's my husband," she said. "I know he can take care of me."

They stood side by side the next morning and watched the wagons pull out. Red-haired Peggy was driving Nathan and Sarah's wagon. Tim looked frightened as he trudged beside his ox team. All the rest—Zer and the silent Martha; whining-voiced Nancy and sharp-eyed George McGee; stolid Bert; fat Joe and Thelma; Ben Metheny who wanted no trouble, and wispy-haired Katherine—none of whom had spoken up—all were headed west into the Tejas Country.

Sarah said in a low voice, "You don't know what made me decide, do you?"

"No—but I'm glad you're here."

"I saw you give two gold pieces to Mother, back at the Falls. They must have been your last."

"We'll be seeing her pretty soon," he said without turning. Peggy, in the second wagon, waved at them, and Sarah waved back. Then she moved close against Nathan, and her hand sought his hand.

CHAPTER XVIII

WOMAN CLAYDON WAS AWAKENED AT DAWN BY THE harsh chatter of a grackle as it pecked some smaller bird to death. He ate a few more persimmons, but when he started to feel sick he threw the rest away. He let the gray crop grass for a few minutes. The horse looked bony; he'd have to get rid of it before he headed for Mexico City.

He rode as far west as he could under cover of the persimmon trees and a scattering of blackjack and sumac. He found a creek bed and got into it. He drank and let the horse drink, his sharp eyes watching in all directions. Then he rode onto higher ground.

A dense fog marked the Sabine. Claydon went into it. He found the road from Natchitoches and followed it cautiously to the river. Here, as at the Mississippi, the riverbanks apparently were higher than the surrounding country, for he crossed a long flat where the road was corduroyed. On his left was a vast bottom filled with cockleburs, and on his right a thick canebrake. He came to a small lean-to made of tall stalks of cane, at the north edge of the road. He dismounted.

"Ho!" he called in a harsh voice, and stood behind the gray, with one hand on his pistol.

There was no answer.

He swept aside the buffalo robe that served as a door. There was a nested-down place in the cane, but no one was sleeping there. Claydon led his horse to the edge of the river.

A quavering voice came out of the fog: *"Aquí, señor, aquí.* This way."

187

Claydon tied the reins around an anchor post. He heard hollow footsteps on wood, then a splat in the mud, and the old voice again, "You wish to cross the river, *señor?*"

Down next to the water the fog was thinner, and Claydon saw the ferryman—an ancient, wizened Spaniard, his hair grayed by many winters, his brown feet bare and wrinkled.

Claydon looked at him coldly. "I seek my brother," he said in Spanish. "A big man, old, red-headed. Eight wagons, many children."

The old Spaniard said, "You do not have red hair, *señor.*"

Claydon's chest began to swell. The *anciano* looked down at the black earth. "I do not see such a many wagon."

Claydon grunted. It had been an idle question anyway, for the train could not have reached the ferry this soon—but one question could lead to another.

"You weesh to cross, *señor?*"

Claydon fixed his beady eyes on the old man. "Where can I find Krudenier?"

"Kruden—" The Spaniard feigned trouble with the unfamiliar sound. He began to shake his head. *"No sabe. No sa—"*

Claydon stuck a knife point into his breastbone. "Where's Krudenier?" he asked coldly.

The old man drew a short breath. He did not cringe nor did he look down at the knife. *"Sí,"* he said finally. "I tell you *en donde.*"

Claydon held the knife hard against the Spaniard's chest. It had cut through the cheap cotton shirt, and now a dark stain began to spread in a small area around the knife point. Claydon kept his black eyes on him.

"Tanto más allá—a little that way," the Spaniard said. He moved only his head—not his eyes or his body.

"Up or down?" Claydon insisted.

"Abajo—down."

"Cuánto?"

"Two leagues, *señor.*"

"What kind of a place?"

"Is a 'dobe—you call 'em sod house."

"Which side of the river?"

"The Tejas side, *señor.*"

Claydon dropped the knife in his boot. Without bending or taking his eyes off the Spaniard, he raised his leg and slipped the knife blade through the guard. "If anybody asks, I have not been here," he said harshly.

"Sí, señor."

The *anciano* seemed withdrawn into himself, behind his ancient black eyes. What he was thinking, Claydon didn't know and didn't care. Maybe, thought Claydon, he is too old to feel pain, but nobody is too old to know fear. "If you talk," Claydon said, "you'll get that knife all the way through."

The *anciano* did not move. His eyes stayed on Claydon's. *"Sí, señor,"* he whispered.

Claydon loped the gray back up the bank to the flat. Then, skirting the cockleburs, he turned downriver to the south. He rode two miles before he came to a sloping bank and put the gray into the water. The Sabine was low except in the middle, and the gray was a good river horse. It came out blowing and started to shake itself, but Claydon was impatient; he slashed it over the eyes with the reins and turned it downstream.

So this was Tejas. It didn't look much different from the Mississippi Territory, with high banks on the river, lakes and swampland along both sides (though these were quite dry now), and beyond them, at a distance from the river, rolling low hills with patches of woods. The lakes that still held water were stagnant, and the air was heavy. The brush near the swampy places was thick enough to stop a good horse unless there was a path.

He worked his way to higher ground. The fog was lifting, and in another hour he came upon a sod hut at the edge of a canebrake. It was a hundred yards from the river, and half that far from the path; cane was thrown carelessly over the roof and against the low walls, and the hut could easily have been missed.

Claydon, without slowing the horse, watched the hut for movement. It was small and square, with walls not over four feet from the ground; the roof was made of cottonwood poles covered with sod and thatched with wild growth. There was one old wooden door and one deerskin window.

Claydon went a hundred yards past, then turned the gray and got off quietly. The old leather didn't creak in the damp air. He walked on the horse's off side back to the hut and hammered on the door with the butt of his pistol. The dry, spongy wood made a dull racket that was enough to rouse a great flock of redwinged blackbirds from the swamp behind the hut. They droned up like a swarm of flies, fighting for room to move their wings. But they settled back almost at once, and Claydon supposed they were eating garbage.

A heavy voice growled, "Whadda ya want?"

"Krudenier," Claydon called, and waited. "I got news from Sam Mason."

The door was pulled in abruptly. *"Entrez,"* growled a heavy voice, and Claydon stepped down into a thick atmosphere that reeked like a ham-curing house—the mark of a chimneyless dwelling.

Claydon saw movement at his right, and realized that Krudenier was covered by somebody else.

"Asseyez-vous, mon ami," said Krudenier.

Claydon sat on a section of log and let his eyes get used to the dimness. Krudenier closed the door, and it seemed like night for a moment. Then a fragrant smell of tobacco came to him.

"You got word from Mason?" asked Krudenier, standing spraddle-legged. He was dressed in what once had been a pair of doeskin breeches, a black shirt open over a hairy chest, and a pair of Indian moccasins.

A lanky Mexican-Indian halfbreed with cinnamon-colored skin and a pronounced hooked nose lay on a buffalo robe, with his head propped against a saddle, smoking a pipe. A pistol protruded from his belt.

"This is news for *you*," said Claydon to the Frenchman. Krudenier answered: "This is Gómez. He's my lieutenant."

"Mason said—" Claydon sensed still more movement in the hut. His eyes darted to the area behind the door. There was a small fire in the open corner, and an Indian woman, her side and back toward Claydon, was blowing up the fire. She was not over nineteen, and Claydon drew in a sudden breath. Her hair was blue-black, short, and parted in the middle. Her arms and legs were strong and gracefully shaped. Her breasts were heavy but firm. And she was entirely naked except for moccasins. The muscles of her back moved like soft steel under velvet-finished mahogany.

"That's my squaw," Krudenier said. "I bought her from a Comanche, but she's really Osage. Her name's Nikaakibuno. In Osage that means She Who Runs to Meet the Men." Krudenier grinned like a good-natured giant. "But don't get any ideas. The first time she runs

191

to meet somebody besides me she knows what will happen."

Claydon finally got his breath. "She—uh—how about her listening?"

"There's only certain words she savvies in English—but you won't be sayin' them words to her."

Claydon, staring at her, realized suddenly there had been a moment's silence after Krudenier's last words. With an effort he forced his gaze away from the Indian girl as she stood up with a knife in one hand and sliced some ribs from a haunch of deer hanging from a cottonwood rafter.

Krudenier's eyes were like flint arrowheads. "All Indian women go around the house like that," he said.

Claydon forced his mind back to Mason's message. "Mason said to tell you there's an eight-wagon train on the way to Natchitoches, headed across the river for Nacogdoches and the Tejas Country. An old man and seven other families. They've got sixty thousand in gold to buy land in Tejas." He waited, watching Krudenier. "They ought to hit the Sabine in about a week."

"Is that all?"

Claydon stared back at the hard gray eyes. "Mason said for me to take his share—one-fourth."

Krudenier studied him deliberately. "I'll deliver one-fourth to you—no more, no less. Women and goods don't count. One-fourth of the money. I'll see that you get it—but I'll not be responsible for what happens to you after you get it. *Comprenez-vous?*"

"I'll be responsible for it after I get it."

"I wonder Mason sent you by yourself. You're big, but you ain't shaped right." He added thoughtfully, "Maybe you're tougher than you look."

Claydon didn't answer.

"Gómez'll put you up at his place till the train gits here," Krudenier said, turning to the Spaniard. "You got room, Gómez?"

"He is welcome to my *palacio*." The voice was soft and silky. Gómez got up; he was very tall. "And there are no *piojos* at my place," he said, watching Krudenier scratch his hairy chest.

Krudenier grunted. "You get a squaw like Nikaakibuno, you'll take the lice and like 'em."

He spun on one heel. The Indian girl had heard her name and stopped her work. She looked up, smiling. When Krudenier spun, she turned back to the fire hurriedly, her hands busy. But Krudenier snatched the pistol from his waistband and slashed her across the bare buttocks with the front sight. Blood welled out and followed the rounded curve to the bottom.

"When I say, 'Git grub,' I mean, 'Git grub!'" Krudenier roared.

Claydon, fascinated, watched the girl. She did not answer, but kept her eyes lowered while she cut off another section of ribs and dropped it into the kettle. Suddenly he knew that Krudenier, punishing the Indian girl, was watching him. He swallowed and forced his eyes away from the woman. Krudenier said nothing. Claydon knew that Krudenier had seen what was in his eyes, but his blood was pounding too hard for him to think about that. He wondered if Krudenier ever left the girl alone in the hut.

Gómez eyed him that night over a bottle of peach brandy he had taken from a murdered immigrant. Gómez lived in a cottonwood log shack about a mile down from Krudenier. His place had a chimney, but the dirt floor reeked with rancid grease. The room was lighted by a candle stuck into its own tallow on the top of a scarred old cherry-wood table that also had come from an immigrant's wagon. "Drink," said Gómez. "There is plenty. She comes through the Zone every day."

Claydon took a big swig and sat there thinking about the Indian girl and Krudenier, up there now in Krudenier's sod hut. His pale forehead began to glisten with sweat.

Gómez filled the tin cup again. *'Por supuesto* you would like to live long enough to take Señor Mason's commission back to him."

Claydon stared at the cinnamon-colored man with the hawk nose, and laughed harshly. "With any luck, I'll live longer than that."

"A fickle thing—is luck."

"What are you drivin' at?"

Gómez' black eyes raised. "Krudenier's squaw," he said in his silky voice.

"I didn't—"

Gómez said blandly: "You have not the impassive face of an Indian or a Mexican, *señor.* Your thoughts are written in your eyes, in your mouth when you look at a woman. Even in the dark hut this morning your eyes have a glitter like a wolf in a cave."

"But Krudenier—"

Gómez tossed the empty bottle into a corner. It hit the cottonwood logs, and a shower of dirt fell from the sod roof. Gómez was getting a little drunk. He stared at the dust that sifted onto the once-fine surface of the red cherry table.

"Krudenier is no *mentecato, amigo*—no fool. He is *hombre de hombres.* He does not get to be general of the Twilight Zone by failing to see what is in a man's

194

heart."

"But a man like him, living like that—" Claydon stopped abruptly. He realized he was revealing his thoughts.

Gómez did not seem to notice. "Others have seen that squaw; others have wanted her. But Krudenier, for all his living in dirt and filth, has his pride. If he invites you to help yourself—and he has done that—that is one thing. But I would not like to be the man who takes her unbidden. Remember, *amigo*, Krudenier gave old Bear That Talks five horses for her."

Claydon took a deep breath. "Yes, I— Five horses!"

Gómez looked up, his head wagging uncertainly. "It's a high price for any woman—but not as high a price as you *might* pay."

He put his long hands flat on the table and got up. He walked unsteadily to a dust-laden bureau with glass doors that bellied out. Then he turned, teetering a little. "You have a very bad fault, amigo. You do not wonder why the other man does as he does. All you concern yourself with is *what* he does. *Ciertamente* you are a fighting man, for Mason would never send any other. But you have not perceive' that Krudenier is a Frenchman." He smiled slowly. "He is *romántico*; and if you tried to take his squaw he'd rather break you in two with his hands than kill you and have it over with. Not like you and me, amigo. *Entiende usted?*"

Claydon was hardly listening. "I guess so," he muttered.

A faint, deep bellow came from somewhere, and Gómez looked up. "You hear that? Krudenier has a landing built for boats that come up from the Gulf with contraband. It is on the river by his place. He has Nikaakibuno throw food into the river there to keep

195

happy El Señor Lagarto—that monster alligator you hear." Gómez cocked an ear. "Why do you suppose he bellows now? Is he looking for a mate to exhaust the energy of his ancient body—or is he hungry for meat scraps?"

Claydon breathed deeply. No answer was called for.

Gómez jerked open one of the glass doors and threw it back hard against the wall. The glass shattered and fell to the dirt floor. Gómez took an earthenware jug from the bureau and stood for a moment, getting his balance.

Claydon drank heavily, but in spite of the liquor the fever in his brain kept him stone-sober.

Gómez eyed him from under lowering lids. "Why you get mixed up in this thing?" he asked. "Why are you the outlaw?"

Claydon tried to get his mind off the squaw. "My father was a riverman on the Susquehanna," he said. "My mother was a waitress in a tavern." He paused. "She left me in a stagecoach and ran off with a coal miner. What else could I do?"

"Is a very fine excuse, *amigo*—but only an excuse. What the man is inside is what he will do. Surroundings do not make a difference. I have been to Castilla, and I tell you that many lovely *señoras* in the Spanish court have lovers more easily than Krudenier's squaw." He looked around the squalid hut with disgust curling his lips. "The bedrooms are different—no dirt dropping from the roof, no rats running across the bed at the moment of ecstasy—but what else is different, amigo?" He pounded the table drunkenly. "Clean us up, or make them filthy—and we are all alike. If a man is made to be a goat, he will be a goat. Inside, people are the same, in the Twilight Zone or in Castilla. Krudenier—he is the

196

only man I know with pride. He lets no man take his squaw—without his permission."

Claydon was still trying to get drunk. Gómez leered. *"No hay nada,"* he mumbled. "There is nothing to worry about. Think no more of Krudenier's squaw. When the big train comes from Natchez, there are seven women. You said so yourself."

Claydon got up and went outside. The night air was damp. The moon was coming up, but a heavy fog was rolling over the valley from the river. Fireflies left brief, glowing trails about waist-high. There were the myriad noises of insects, a constant croaking of bullfrogs, the weird hooting of an owl far off in the swamp, and, from somewhere up above, the deep, thumping bellow of the bull alligator. Claydon slapped at a mosquito. He heard the alligator bellow again, and faced upstream for a moment. Krudenier's place was in that direction, but there was no indication of a light, for between them lay a great point of swamp and canebrake. Claydon turned slowly and went back inside. Gómez was asleep on a pile of buffalo robes in a corner. Claydon found a robe, kicked some bottles out of another corner, and lay down. The candle flickered. Claydon got up and blew it out. Yes, there were women with the wagon train. Maybe Krudenier would like one of those women for a while. Claydon felt suddenly feverish again. A man couldn't very well be in two places at once.

CHAPTER XIX

CLAYDON WOULD HAVE STAYED AWAY FROM Krudenier's place if he could have—and he would have gone oftener if he could have. As it was, he didn't see Nikaakibuno again for three days.

Gómez went up there every day, and sometimes was gone most of the night, but he never reported on those excursions.

Claydon, in the meantime, scouted up and down the river. He went up as far as Krudenier's place and saw the rough wooden boat landing. He looked for a long time at Krudenier's sod hut, but Nikaakibuno did not appear. He walked back along the path to Gómez' place, and all the way he could hear the whomping bass-voiced bellow of Señor Lagarto.

There seemed to be considerable traffic from every direction to Krudenier's place, and Gómez explained it one morning while they sat playing old sledge.

"Krudenier, he give' the orders for all looting on the Old Spanish Road across the Zone," he said, "especially in Tejas on the Nacogdoches side. Nobody robs a single wagon without Krudenier says so." Suddenly Gómez scattered a handful of dirty cards over the floor. "Why was I born part Apache?" he demanded. "Why must I rob and kill and play cards with a maniac like you?"

Claydon drew back watchfully. Gómez' sudden moods were not reassuring.

"*Por Dios*, you are crazy!" Gómez said. "Woman-crazy. You have seen Krudenier's squaw and you think you must have her and her only." He shook his head. "It is *no bueno*."

Claydon moistened his lips. "I don't—"

Gómez had his left forefinger in the hook at the neck of the rum jug. He swung the jug up on his arm and held it high while he put his mouth to the opening. He looked up. "Krudenier, he knows, and he is wait' for you to make a move." Gómez stared at Claydon through bleary eyes. "It does not change your mind, *amigo.* You are determine'. But I am tell' you that one Indian squaw is not only the most desirable woman in all Tejas; she is also the most dangerous woman in the Zone. Krudenier does not mind your looking, but he will kill you if you touch her—and kill you slow, with his hands."

Gómez took another drink; the liquor gurgled noisily in his throat. He raised his head a little and his eyes still more, and looked upriver, and then, for the first time, Claydon knew that Gómez himself lusted for Nikaakibuno. However, he did not think Gómez would try to take her; the halfbreed had not the courage to face Krudenier.

Gómez seemed to pull his mind away from the squaw with an effort. "Krudenier tells everybody not to bother the immigrants on the Louisiana side till your train comes through. He is afraid stories get back to Natchitoches and scare them away."

Claydon nodded. "That's a good thing." He asked, "Has he got scouts looking for the train?"

"The old man at the ferry." Gómez slammed the jug on the table. "He will delay the wagons while he gets word to Krudenier."

"How can he send word?"

"A fire, a few green cottonwood leaves."

Claydon considered. "How much does the *anciano* get?" he asked.

"Him? Maybe *cien pesos*—a hundred dollars. Maybe less, maybe more." Gómez shrugged. "Sometimes

199

maybe Krudenier gets drunk and pays him twice."

Claydon looked at Gómez. "What would an *anciano* do with that much money?"

"He is save his money to buy a few sheep and a piece of land out in Nuevo Méjico. Why not? He is too old to spend his money on the *señoritas*. He might as well raise sheep."

Claydon said slowly, "Maybe."

Gómez lurched out through the open door. "We go up to Krudenier's place now and he tells us his plans."

Claydon got up swiftly. With a loaded pistol in his waist, his knife in his boot, and his rifle in his hands, he walked up the path after Gómez. Outside Krudenier's place the carcass of a black bear hung by its hind legs from the low limb of a big cottonwood. The animal had been gutted and skinned, and the head was gone. The hide was piled on the grass and a buzzard floated overhead. Gómez observed, "Somebody gets tired of deer meat, eh?"

The carcass swung a little in the hot wind, but not enough to disturb the flies attracted by the blood.

Seeing two horses standing ground-hitched outside the door, they knew that Krudenier had company. Gómez pushed in without knocking, and Claydon followed.

Krudenier was standing near the deerskin window, his black shirt open over his hairy chest, his black whiskers tangled. Two pots were over the fire, both simmering. In one of them was cooking the bear's head, whole. Four other men were in the small hut with its overpowering odor of baked ham. One was an Indian, naked from waist up, with a tomahawk at his belt. One was a small man, almost a midget, with eyes as cold and unfeeling as those of Bloody Harpe. The third had a black pad over one eye in a square face, and a blue kerchief wrapped around his head. The fourth was a big Negro. Claydon looked for the squaw as soon as his eyes got used to the dimness. She came in the door and went past them. His gaze dwelt feverishly on her solid, heavy breasts and her firm round buttocks. The other men also watched her as she went by, but said nothing. She got a butcher knife and went back out. The long welt where Krudenier had slashed her showed plainly in the sunlight. Krudenier grinned at Claydon and scratched his chest.

"The train got into Natchitoches night before last, and they left yesterday," Krudenier said to all of them. "There is this old man, seven families, three servants, and a guide they picked up in Natchez." Krudenier slid a knife out of its sheath at his side and fished in one of the simmering pots until he came up with a couple of boiled ribs. "The guide is in my pay," he said, skinning the greasy meat off the bone with his teeth.

"How many men do we use?" asked the little man.

"Thirty-two. We might do it with less, but it's a big train and I don't want to take any chances." Both of his hands were full of meat. He turned to the little man. "Pequeño, you'll have eight men in the canebrake on this side of the crossing. We'll wait till they are split up on both sides of the river. One-Eye will go in first, as soon as I start fighting on the other side, and you will back up One-Eye." He glanced at the black. "Raoul and I will meet in the slough; we'll split, and one party will go on each side of the train. And you, Yellow Knife—" The Indian's face was like stone. "Keep your Choctaws behind the cane above the ferry on the other side. After the fight starts, lead your warriors down, yelling like fiends out of hell." Krudenier grinned, but his gray eyes were cold. "Then everybody attack. They won't know which way to turn."

Yellow Knife looked at Krudenier. *"Hakchuma cho? Wishki cho?"*

"There'll be plenty tobacco and plenty whisky—*anumpa kallo ilonuchi*. I promise."

Yellow Knife nodded gravely. *"Nakni pokoli amala cho?"*

"That's right. Ten warriors." He spoke to the other three. "Pick your men well. An old man who has made that much money does not give it up without a fight."

One-Eye nodded slowly. Raoul's eyes were white in his black face. Pequeño studied Krudenier. "When do we divide the money?" he asked.

Krudenier tossed the bones into a corner and ran his greasy fingers over his head till his black hair glistened with bear oil. "We'll split the money while the men are celebrating. *C'est très bien, n'est-ce pas?"*

"Bien," said Pequeño.

Krudenier turned to Claydon and finished wiping his fingers on his doeskin breeches. "You'll be with me and Gómez. You want to see that Mason gets his share, don't you?"

Claydon didn't like the way Krudenier looked at him—not quite straight. "I'll be there," Claydon said, and then, thinking to impress them all and make it easier for him to ride away with his share of gold without getting a bullet in his back, went on, "Old Mason would wrap my guts around my legs and feed me to the alligators if I didn't bring his share back to him."

"You think that's a bad way to die?" Krudenier asked quickly.

Claydon frowned. The Frenchman had a way of making him uncomfortable. "Would *any*body like it?"

202

Claydon asked finally.

"Maybe not so," said Krudenier. "I have done better myself, I think, but every man is entitled to his own opinion."

On the next day the wagon train camped about five leagues from the Sabine, obviously planning to get an early start next morning so that they could make the crossing and camp on the Tejas side that evening. Gómez emptied two pistols at a heavy-winged white crane, and reloaded them with fresh powder. He sharpened two knives on a sickle stone. "You like to whet yours?" he asked Claydon.

"My knife is always sharp," Claydon said.

Gómez looked at him strangely. He spat on the stone and spread the saliva carefully with his forefinger. Then he began to work the knife back and forth, turning it each time to feed the edge into the stone. "It is better you stay close to me tomorrow," he said.

The sun was still an hour above the canebrake to the west when Gómez took a last drink from the rum jug. "Let us go, *amigo*. Krudenier will not like it if we are late."

They saddled their horses and rode up the path. A cloud of blackbirds buzzed up like flies ahead of them. Gómez was carrying the jug. "It is empty," he told Claydon as they came in sight of Krudenier's place. "If you come with me to the boat landing, I show you something."

Claydon remained seated on his horse on the bank while Gómez dismounted and walked out on the landing, his boots making hollow sounds on the planks. The river was low and the water was clear. Gómez swung the empty jug back and then forward. It sailed out over the water and seemed to pause, then dropped with a great splash. Almost instantly the water boiled, and then a huge, greenish-black, moss-covered back arched for an instant, breaking the water. The saurian turned as it struck, showing a dead-white belly. There was a great swirl, and through the turbulence an immense dark shape drifted toward the opposite shore and out of sight.

Gómez chuckled. "El Señor Lagarto will be most unhappy when he finds out he has swallow' an empty rum jug. No?" He looked straight at Claydon. For an instant his eyes did not seem bleary—or was it Claydon's imagination? "We feed him well after we get through with the wagon train, *verdad? Tal vez* somebody weel kill a bear, no?"

Claydon did not smile. He looked at the sardonic mouth under the hawk nose, and for the first time he knew how easy it would be for the Twilighters to stop him from leaving. Krudenier had promised to deliver the gold—but that was all. Claydon compressed his lips. Many men would know how much gold he was carrying. His small eyes watched Gómez' back as they went on to Krudenier's. A knife between Gómez' shoulder blades—but Claydon didn't even know if Gómez was the one to fear.

There were three horses outside Krudenier's—a bay and a sorrel, their reins on the ground, their high Spanish saddles worn and shabby, and Krudenier's horse, a close-coupled grullo, fifty feet away, hunting a few eatable blades of grass and switching his tail against the bottleflies.

The grullo looked like a good horse, Claydon noticed. His own gray had fattened up somewhat in the several days he had been at the Sabine, but a gray marked him too much. He wondered if that was why Mason had sent him on the gray—so that he could keep track of him. Claydon looked over the other two. They weren't much, but he wasn't worried. There'd be plenty of opportunity to grab a couple of good horses—one to ride and one to lead—while Krudenier's gang was celebrating the wagon-train massacre. He'd make a quick trip back to Krudenier's cabin, then on down the Sabine for a few leagues. He had scouted the river and knew the way. He could turn due west and hit the Spanish Road to San Antonio de Béjar, avoiding Nacogdoches entirely. They'd never look for him that way. Neither would Mason. They all expected him to go back to Natchitoches. The way through Tejas would be clear, and Mexico City, with its many beautiful women, was at the end of the road.

Claydon felt more assured when he stepped down into the smoky atmosphere of Krudenier's place. Krudenier, his black shirt open to the waist as usual, was waving a brown bottle in a big hand. The one-eyed pirate sat hunched in a corner, his head drawn in between his shoulders, his eye red and bloodshot. Pequeño, the little man, was sitting straight at the homemade log table, a bottle before him, his eyes cold and watchful. The Indian girl sat on the floor before the fire. Meat was simmering in the big iron pot, and the thin smoke from damp cottonwood sticks rose around the pot in a wavering curtain that broke when it got to the ceiling and filled the top of the room with a blue haze.

Claydon glanced once at the girl, then took his eyes away from her—but not soon enough. Krudenier's eyes were squarely on him, and Krudenier wasn't grinning.

Claydon said abruptly, "I'm figuring to start back as soon as it's over."

Krudenier waited a long time before answering. "So

maybe if you don' get back soon old Mason will come after you, *n'est-ce pas?*"

Claydon tried to look like a man acting unconcerned. "He's too busy along the Trace to come over here."

"There are many people coming down from the Western Country, now that Louisiana belongs to the United States?"

"Plenty. And most of them have money."

"One thing I do not understand. If Mason knew this old man had so much money, why didn't Mason attack the train near Natchez?"

Claydon realized that the cabin was quiet except for the slow bubbling of the meat in the iron pot. He looked at Krudenier. "Mason is in bad with the Spanish commandant at Fort Concordia and he has no passport."

The lids dropped over the upper halves of Krudenier's gray eyes. He took a drink from the bottle, but his gaze did not leave Claydon. "It better go right."

Claydon recognized a threat when he heard one. The commission arrangement between Krudenier and Mason was precarious at best, and Krudenier would welcome any excuse to keep a one-fourth share of so much money from going back to Natchez. Claydon glanced at the suspicious eyes of Pequeño, at the bloodshot eye of the pirate, at the sardonic eyes of Gómez, lying on the buffalo robe, and finally back at the hard, uncompromising gray eyes of Krudenier. "Why should it go wrong?" Claydon asked. "How can Mason make any money if it goes wrong?"

The tension broke. Krudenier thumped the bottle on the table and said, *"Avant!"*

Gómez got up slowly from the buffalo robe, his gaze lingering on Nikaakibuno. Pequeño came from behind the table. The pirate got up. He was almost hunchbacked, but he had powerful shoulders and long, reaching arms. Krudenier followed them and went ahead of Claydon. Krudenier ducked his head as he went through the door, and Claydon realized for the first time how deceptively big the man was. He wasn't heavy anywhere; he tapered from the chest down, and there was a quickness and a smoothness in his movements that was a warning.

Claydon flicked a last glance at the Indian girl. She was gazing into the fire, but as Claydon looked at her she seemed to feel his intensity, for she turned her head slightly toward him, and her white eyes rolled upward. It lasted only an instant; then she looked back at the fire.

Claydon took a deep breath and stepped up out of the hut.

The hundred tight curls of Krudenier's greasy black hair gleamed in the last rays of the yellowing sun. "We'll cross up here a couple of miles," he said to Gómez. "You two, Pequeño and One-Eye, see that your men are in place. Watch me and don't attack until I do."

Pequeño nodded, his eyes bright as polished agate. One-Eye grunted. They got on their horses and rode away.

Krudenier swung into the saddle of the grullo and set off after them. Claydon and Gómez followed. Krudenier turned right and waded the grullo into the river.

The horses shook themselves when they got out of the water. Claydon's Holland-cloth pants were soaked and his boots were full of water, but there was no time to stop. They picked up six armed men at the bottom of a dry slough. Raoul, the black man, and his party rode up alongside.

Krudenier led them at a trot upriver to the ferry, where they came out on the flat.

CHAPTER XX

THREE JERSEY WAGONS IN BLUE PAINT, WITH CANVAS turning gray, each pulled by four oxen, were waiting in line on the east side of the river, along with eighteen or twenty extra oxen. One wagon was on the ferry in the middle of the river, and four wagons, also with extra oxen, already were on the other side. Two women and several children stood at the edge of the river on the other side; on the near side, all were in their wagons. On the ferry, a man in knee-length scuffed boots and a red wool shirt turned the crank that moved the ferry slowly to the Tejas side, while the *anciano* sat on the edge of the raft, dangling his wrinkled brown feet in the water.

Krudenier, followed by his men in single file, rode along the north side of the string of three wagons; Raoul and his men rode along the south. The sun had gone out of sight and left a weird half-light over the river. Krudenier rode up to a big man with grizzled red whiskers and a wide-brimmed black hat, who was holding the brake on the first wagon.

A woman's shrill voice came from the first wagon. "Pa, do you think we'll get across by dark?"

"Don't worry," the big man said. "We'll all be across in no time, now that the ferry's going again."

"Trouble, mister?" asked Krudenier.

The old man was a fierce-eyed old cuss, Claydon saw.

"We been here most of the afternoon." He sounded disgusted, like a man who was used to having things go right. "This ferry's a joke. I thought the Spanish government required them to keep up the ferries on the Camino Real."

Krudenier raised his eyebrows. "The government is fifteen hundred miles away," he said.

The old man had looked over Krudenier's crew by that time, and he obviously didn't like what he saw. With his hand still on the brake, he swung back against the front wheel to watch the slow progress of the ferry.

Krudenier crowded him. "How much money have you got?"

The old man's eyes blazed. "I won't be blackmailed," he shouted, "to get across any river in the world!"

"It isn't blackmail," said Krudenier. "It isn't a ferry fee. It's robbery. We want your money. You'll save lives if you turn it over peaceful."

A long rifle was thrust from under the canvas at the side of the wagon. "Get away!" said the shrill voice. "I'll shoot."

Krudenier swung to one side. His big knife ripped the canvas down between the hoops, and he grinned at the sharp-nosed woman in a light blue bonnet who now struggled to get the long rifle free of the canvas.

Krudenier's big fingers took hold of the rifle and threw it back over his head. The old man swung on him with a pistol, but Krudenier rode him down with the grullo. The pistol went off, but the old man was on his back with the grullo's hoofs in his face, and his shot hit an ox in the rump. The bull bellowed and surged forward. The brake was off now, and the wagon rolled toward the water, crowding the heels of the oxen. The woman screamed. A shot came from the wagon. Children began to wail.

The heavy front wheel of the wagon stopped against the old man's body. Then the bulls lurched into their yokes, the big chain tightened, and the steel tire went across the old man's chest with a steady crunching of bone. But the old man was as hard to kill as a buffalo bull. He roared up before the hind wheel got to him, with a knife in his hand.

One of Krudenier's men on the far side of the wagon grabbed the woman. She fought like a badger. Krudenier saw the old man coming after him, and shot him between the eyes.

The Twilighter who had hold of the woman suddenly released her and dropped back. The side of his neck was like a bloody mushroom. He fell at full length from his horse, and the woman dived back under the canvas.

Shots came from across the river. Pequeño and One-Eye and their men were attacking the four wagons on that side. Hoarse shouts and strangled cries floated across the Sabine.

The ferry had stopped. The man who had been turning the crank was on his knees, reloading. It must have been he who had shot the Twilighter through the neck. The ancient Spaniard also was on his knees, crossing himself.

Gómez grasped Krudenier's shoulder and pointed. Krudenier looked at the dead outlaw on the other side of the wagon, then at the ferry, and his eyes narrowed. He jumped the grullo down to the edge of the water and hacked at the rope with his knife. The rope parted with a small crackling noise. The ferry lurched and swung downstream.

It would swing against the opposite bank, too far away for a rifle shot to the Louisiana side, and screened from the site of the attack on the Tejas side by a thick growth of mulberry trees. Krudenier wheeled back. Those still alive in the two wagons left on the Louisiana side had forted up and were firing.

"Burn the canvas!" Krudenier shouted.

One man went off to one side and got down on the ground with a flint and steel. A rifle spoke from one of the wagons and he went over on his back, sprawled out. Krudenier roared, "Cut the bulls loose!"

But the outlaws were beginning to hunt cover. The firing from the wagons was slow but steady. "They must have half a dozen guns in every wagon," Krudenier growled.

The first wagon had rolled into the water and was now bed-deep. The oxen, in to their briskets, stood calmly, but the woman leaped from the canvas at the rear with a child under each arm. She waded toward shore. A black-haired, sharp-eyed man came immediately after her with an ax in his hands.

Gómez grinned. He rode down to the edge of the water, wheeled his horse, and shot the man in the chest. The man staggered. His arms dropped. Gómez turned his horse into the water and made a pass at him with a knife.

"Look out, he's got a pistol!" Krudenier shouted.

But the man wasn't pointing the pistol at Gómez. He held it on the woman, but hesitated. She turned her breast to him and smiled. "Hurry, George!" He pulled the trigger, and she went under the water at the same time as he did, with the children held firmly in her arms.

Gómez' face turned black. *"Hija de chingada!"* he screamed. "She was young, too!" He rode his horse back and forth over their bodies.

Someone had a fire going, and threw a burning stick at a wagon. Raoul rode by with a blazing bundle of dry grass and threw it in one end of the wagon. The canvas began to burn, but still a shot came from under the edge.

Then a chorus of hideous yells rolled down over the canebrake. Yellow Knife's Choctaws were coming.

211

Their ponies burst through the canebrake, and the half naked, painted Choctaws swept around the two wagons in a circle, shrieking war cries.

There seemed to be a moment's hesitation from the two wagons. The canvas on both was blazing fiercely. There was a shot—two shots. Then a man appeared from each. One, who resembled the old man but was too fat, had a grubbing hoe in his hands; the other, a light-haired, timid-looking man, had a spare singletree. They came face to face with Yellow Knife's Choctaws, and both fell, their bodies bristling with feathered shafts.

A loud, strong voice arose in song: "Lawd, I'se comin' home."

Raoul galloped up to the side of the wagon. "You!" he shouted, "come outa theah!"

The song continued: "My soul is sick, my heart is sore; now I'se coming home."

A ten-year-old boy jumped from the back end of the wagon and started to run for the cane. A Choctaw tomahawk split his head open.

Gómez leaped from his horse and picked up the grubbing hoe. He cut off the canvas-hoops on one side of a wagon. Krudenier threw a rope over and drew off the whole burning mass. Gómez ran to the front of the wagon and jumped up on the wagon pole. Then he swore again: "Santa Maria! They shot another woman!"

Claydon watched. So far he hadn't fired his pistol; he might need it later—and "later" was getting close.

The dead woman, a young one with golden hair, had fallen on her baby in such a way that it had smothered under the folds of her dress. Gómez, disgusted, went to the last wagon. The song was still coming up from the middle of the blaze. "Get her out of there!" he screamed at Raoul. "They're killing each other. She's the only woman left!"

Raoul vaulted from his horse. A big Negro woman arose from the middle of the fire, still singing. Her clothes were burning; the red kerchief that covered her hair was aflame, but her voice was still loud and strong: "Oh, wash me whiter than the snow; Lord, I'se coming home."

Krudenier grunted. "She's no good," and put a bullet in her.

The Choctaws were working on the bodies. An Indian would make a cut around a skull, brace one foot on chest or back, and jerk off the scalp in one swift movement.

Gómez began to search the wagons. He found another dead woman—a young fat one. Two of Raoul's black men cleared the canvas and hoops from the second wagon, and threw burning goods to the ground—some comforters, three bolts of cloth, an Eastern saddle, an extra tarp. Raoul let out a yell: "Two kegs of whisky in heah!"

Krudenier sent two Choctaws across the river to get the man on the ferry. The sun was down and it would be dark before long. Gómez reported, "There is nada worth having but the two kegs of rye."

"Take the rye and burn the wagons," said Krudenier. "What about the bulls?"

"The Choctaws'll get them later. Maybe they get tired of horse meat sometimes. Let's go across the river and see what luck Pequeño and One-Eye had."

They splashed across on their horses. It wasn't deep enough to require swimming. One of the four wagons was a huge bonfire surrounded by destruction and death. Pequeño's men cut the bulls loose, and the Choctaws went after the lumbering beasts with drawn knives.

213

Yellow Knife rode alongside a big bull. As he reached the animal's flank, his knife rose and fell about its withers. The bull piled up on its front legs. Yellow Knife slashed at the bull's loin, then buried his arm to the elbow in the jerking body. He worked for a minute, and then the bloody arm came out, his fingers clutching a huge piece of dripping liver. He held it in both hands and bit into it, while the blood ran down his arms.

Krudenier rode up to the fire, still bareheaded, a magnificent figure in his black shirt, with the yellow light of the burning wagon shining on the black curls that covered his head. "What did you get?" he asked Pequeño.

The little man pointed. "There is a leathern bag under the seat of the fourth wagon. We have not opened it." His sharp eyes watched Krudenier.

"What else?"

"Six bundles of Virginia tobacco, four kegs of Kentucky whisky, some flour, bacon, cornmeal, coffee, sugar, salt, a hogshead full of dishes—"

"You idiot!" whispered Gómez. *"How many women did you take?"*

"One," said Pequeño, and turned his sharp eyes on Gómez. "The rest are all dead. They killed each other at the last."

"Where's the one?" demanded Gómez.

"Over there by the second wagon," said Pequeño. "This was a red-haired one—the last one left. She tried to kill herself."

"One's better than none," said Gómez, his eyes gleaming beside his hawk nose.

"If you can make love to a woman with half her head shot off," said Pequeño.

Claydon became aware of a low moaning sound.

Gómez glared down at Pequeño. He stared at the pirate's bloodshot eye. Then he went to the second wagon, stopped, and snorted in disgust. His knife appeared in his hand. He stooped, and the moaning stopped. Gómez swore. He threw over a hogshead, and Claydon heard the tinkling of broken dishes.

There was a shot from the direction of the ferry, then a heavy splash as if a body had fallen into the water. Krudenier looked up, nodded slightly. He strode to the pile of goods. Four men lifted the leather bag to the center of the pile. Krudenier smiled. He sliced off the top with an ax, and the bag spread like a huge flower, with gold eagles and half-eagles clinking softly against one another. Krudenier took a deep breath and glanced at Claydon. "Mason was right."

Claydon's small eyes watched Krudenier. Very soon now his own time would come and, he thought, the sooner the better. When these men got drunk, anything might happen. He had it in mind to suggest that Krudenier divide the gold immediately, but he remembered that Pequeño, too, was interested in the money, and he kept his mouth shut.

"Pull the wagons together," said Krudenier, "and burn 'em. We'll need light."

Men put their backs and shoulders to the wheels of the wagons. They rolled them against the already burning pyre, and left them, bodies and all.

A shout went up. The ancient Spaniard was coming up the trail from the ferry on foot.

"Give Pablo the wine," said Krudenier, and the *anciano's* old eyes brightened as he trotted up to receive his share of the liquor.

Krudenier parceled out the food, the tobacco, and the whisky, while the men began to draw closer and be quieter. "We'll give plenty whisky to the Choctaws," Krudenier said. "Then they won't care about the money."

Claydon got in a little nearer. The bag of gold coins, as big as a washtub, lay in the middle, and the outlaws began to watch it and nothing else.

Then Gómez found a tin cup and filled it half full of whisky. He took the jug of wine from Pablo and finished filling the cup to the brim. He took a long drink and shouted to the men: "Don't be so damn' sober. You can't drink money and you can't make love to it."

But Gómez failed to stir them. They gathered in a tighter circle, glitter-eyed, waiting for Krudenier to get down to business.

Only the Choctaws were unconcerned. They took their keg of whisky to a big pecan tree and sat down to serious drinking. Krudenier roared, "Let's ev'rybody have a drink!" He filled a cup for himself and stood with his big hand on the spigot. "Ev'rybody! *Tout le monde!*"

They filed by slowly. Most of them tossed off their half-cupful at once. Claydon looked into Krudenier's face as the liquor ran into his cup. There was a quizzical look in the Frenchman's opaque eyes that Claydon didn't like.

"It was a successful raid, *mon ami*," said Krudenier. "If you can get back through the Avoyelles country to Natchez, you are safe, *n'est-ce pas?*"

Claydon nodded. He was worried. They had not captured a woman, and that changed the situation. He had counted on their being occupied for a while. But now there was only one thing sure: there would be trouble tonight—bad trouble. Men long without women and unexpectedly deprived of them got ugly. Claydon

216

emptied his cup and set it down.

Krudenier began to parcel out the goods.

An hour later, by the glowing light of the wagons' ashes, Krudenier was counting the gold, and the men were getting very drunk. Krudenier sat cross-legged, the firelight on his black-haired chest, a tin cup of whisky at his side. Krudenier was getting a little drunk himself, but he put every fourth coin into a separate pile. Finally he stood up. "Sixty-one thousand and some-odd. We have divide' one-fourth to Mason according to the agreement. I will take a third for me and my men. The rest is divide' up between Pequeño, One-Eye, and Raoul. *Bien?*"

Pequeño nodded, his eyes filled with the gold—his mind, probably, filled with the thought of strutting in Nacogdoches or Natchitoches with the power of the gold behind him. Pequeño was a little man, and the gold would be important to him. One-Eye reached out a big hand and sifted coins through his fingers. Raoul stood a little back, like a crystallization of the shadows along the river, his eyes very white in his black face.

Pequeño said impatiently to Krudenier, "Take yours." Krudenier divided the three-fourths part into three piles, and motioned Gómez to put one pile into an *alforja.* "That's for me." He looked up, his gray eyes enigmatical. "You want to split the rest?" he asked Pequeño.

"You," said One-Eye. "Divide it fair and square."

Krudenier began to count again. Presently he was finished, and Pequeño, One-Eye, and Raoul took their shares and drew off to divide with their men.

Claydon put his gold in his packsaddle and threw it on the gray. He turned back and said, "Now let's have another drink." One-Eye held a fistful of gold over his head. "Let's go to Nacogdoches," he roared. "There's women there!"

Pequeño's serious face loosened up. "Let's go to Nacogdoches," he said.

"Nacogdoches!" shouted Krudenier, lurching to his feet. Claydon mounted his horse, and tension filled his chest. "You coming?" asked Krudenier.

Claydon shook his head. "Not me. I'm heading for Natchez tonight."

Krudenier's eyes widened as if he was surprised. "Tonight? You're in a big hurry, *mon ami.*"

Claydon tried to grin. "With the country full of cutthroats like these, do you blame me?" He added for effect, "Mason will be waiting for his share."

One-Eye staggered up and laid his hand on the mane of Claydon's horse. "How much that you get yourself?" he asked thickly. Claydon said slowly, carefully, "I get a hundred dollars."

"You work too damn' cheap," One-Eye growled, but he backed off, and Claydon drew his breath again. *"Adiós,"* he said, and turned the horse.

CHAPTER XXI

THE GRAY HAD TAKEN THREE STEPS TOWARD THE river when a voice called, *"Un momento!"*

For an instant Claydon froze. Then he recognized the *anciano.* "Sí?" he answered.

"You will take me across? I no can swim—and the ferry—she's busted."

"Sure," said Claydon. "Climb up behind." At least the old man could stop bullets.

He let the Spaniard use his stirrup. The old man hung onto his jug of wine with his right hand. He seated himself on the skirt of the saddle and turned the jug up for another pull. As he lowered it, Claydon pushed the gray into the water.

"Attendez-vous!" Krudenier roared.

For an instant Claydon was panicky. The pressure in his throat was almost choking him. He could dump the *anciano* at the first jump, but there was the gold. It weighed a hundred pounds, and the gray was still somewhat run down from the trip across Louisiana. He wouldn't have much chance to get away. They'd have his back full of bullets before he reached the middle of the river. In the dark he loosened the pistol at his waist and turned the gray back at the edge of the water.

"We didn't pay Pablo," said Krudenier. "You"—he pointed to Pequeño—"a gold piece for our good friend. And you, Raoul—One-Eye—"

Gómez collected the money and brought it to the Spaniard, who took it in the claws of his ancient hand and mumbled, *"Mil gracias. Mil gracias."*

Gómez looked up at Claydon in the dim glow from

219

the embers of the wagon. "You start now, *amigo?* It is a long ride to Natchitoches at night. You better go with us to Nacogdoches, and you can start home in the morning."

Claydon's chest seemed about to explode. He tried to expel his breath without noise. "Mason will be looking for me." Then he rode the gray splashing into the water, not fast enough to suggest that he was running, not slow enough to give them time to think.

In a moment he was beyond the dim light of the fire. The gray, cautious under its heavy burden, felt its way across the stream. Claydon heard the outlaws lining out their horses for the ride to Nacogdoches, and looked back. The Indians were asleep under the pecan tree, and Gómez was mounting his horse. Claydon recognized his silhouette against the fire.

The gray pulled out of the river alongside the ferry landing. Claydon said, "Down, *viejo.*"

The old man climbed down. Claydon didn't offer him the stirrup again, and the Spaniard fell to the ground, still clutching the wine jug. Claydon heard him scraping the dirt with his fingers—probably for his money. "Women I like," the old Spaniard mumbled, "but twenty leagues to Nacogdoches is too far to ride on a night when one is tired."

He stumbled to his cane lean-to. Claydon watched him go inside. The outlaws were riding out to the west, and from the head of the column came the roar of Krudenier's voice as he led the way. Claydon moved off slowly. The *anciano* seemed, by the sounds, to fall into his bunk and stay there without moving. Claydon rode to the top of the rise. He sat the gray in the dark for some time, until the voices of the outlaws faded out toward Nacogdoches. Whatever intentions any of them had toward him, he thought, were of no account now. They'd never suspect that he was going to cross the river again into Tejas.

Claydon waited a little longer. The moon came up and illuminated the weird wreaths of fog that arose from the river. Presently Claydon rode back to the lean-to. The Spaniard was snoring. Claydon pulled open the buffalo-robe door. He reached in and seized the old man's vest with his fingers. He shook him and growled, "Where's the money?"

The *anciano* mumbled, "Nacogdoches is *más allá*— too far." Claydon dragged him out. He wasn't very heavy. Claydon lifted the cane that formed the *anciano's* bed, and felt underneath. There was a small covered pit there. He tore the twigs away and reached down. Then he drew a deep breath. The *anciano* had enough to buy a sheep ranch, all right. Claydon scooped it out. He put the coins in his saddlebag. He guessed there was maybe two thousand dollars—a good night's work.

The old man pawed him. "You take my pesos," he said, and his voice was panicky. "I save' them for *muchos anos*—many years. I am save' them to buy a few sheep when I am old. You take my pesos. You cannot do this—"

Claydon slid his knife between the *anciano's* ribs. The Spaniard crumpled. He was old anyway. Claydon stepped over his body and stood for a moment, listening. He heard frogs, crickets, nighthawks. He no longer heard any sound from Krudenier's men. The Choctaws across the river were still asleep, and the fire was glowing less and less.

The moon was edging over the mulberry trees. Claydon mounted the gray and walked it back up the rise. He turned downriver and rode quietly. The cane was still green and did not make too much noise. He reached the ford where Krudenier had crossed, and went into the water. On the Tejas side he stopped, thinking. The outlaws' departure for Nacogdoches had taken away the horses—all but those of the Choctaws. And they were dead drunk.

He tied up the gray very quietly and securely. If a bobcat scared the horse, he didn't want it running away with all that gold. He went up the path, as cat-footed as any Indian. Fireflies winked on and off before him. He passed the swinging ferry with the wagon still on it. He came to the clearing. The embers made only a faint glow. He stood in the dark at the edge of the clearing for five minutes, searching the shadows, listening. Finally he walked around the clearing, keeping under the trees, making no noise. He found an Indian asleep with a rawhide rein rope twisted around his hand. Claydon cut the rope next to the Indian's hand and led the horse away.

The gray was like a landmark in the moonlight. He tied the Indian horse's rein to a ring on his saddle, mounted the gray, and rode down the path toward Krudenier's. Krudenier must be well on his way to Nacogdoches by now.

The sod hut sat there in the moonlight, with just a little fog rolling across the low spot from the river. Claydon dismounted and moistened his lips. He went to the door of the hut and stood there an instant, listening. He looked behind but saw nothing. Then he could stand it no longer. He hit the door with his shoulder.

It gave way. He stepped down inside, his eyes searching the blackness. He felt movement, and knew the Osage girl was before him. He reached for her. His fingers found the bare flesh that was like warm velvet. He looked down and saw her eyes, like dark islands in white pools. As he started to push her over, a big hand was laid on his shoulder and he was pulled back through the door. He spun, snatching at his pistol.

Krudenier stood before him, his shirt open at the waist, his black hair in tight curls that glistened even in the moonlight.

"You are the tricky dog," Krudenier said slowly. "But I know you want my squaw, so I am not fool' when you cross the river. I leave the others and circle back here to wait for you."

Krudenier was moving around him, and Claydon was scared. He didn't think the man had a pistol, but suddenly he knew what Gómez had tried to tell him: Krudenier was a man afraid of nothing.

The moon was in Claydon's eyes, and though he wanted to turn, he didn't dare. Krudenier, three feet away, was watching him like a cat. Claydon hesitated to draw his pistol, and in that hesitation he recognized his own lack of confidence. What kind of man was this Krudenier anyway? Unarmed, apparently, he was not afraid of Claydon, who had his hand on his pistol butt. Worse, Claydon saw in an instant of panic, Krudenier wanted it that way. As Gómez had said, the Frenchman would not be satisfied merely to get rid of Claydon; he wanted to mangle him with his hands.

Krudenier was stalking him, his eyes fixed on Claydon's. It was a warm night, and the hum of insects rose from the canebrake. Sweat began to roll down Claydon's forehead. He tried again to get his back to the moon, but the other wouldn't let him. He had a glimpse of the Osage girl in the open doorway. The upper half of her bronze body, unclothed, seemed to glow in the moonlight; the lower half was in shadow.

Krudenier kept edging closer. Claydon kept backing. Then he felt the pistol beneath his hand, and, his panic over, he knew there was nothing about Krudenier a pistol would not take care of. Claydon snatched the weapon out of his waistband. At the same time Krudenier leaped.

Claydon pulled the trigger as the man left the ground, and heard the bullet smack into the big Frenchman's body. Then Krudenier was on him like a Mississippi tornado. The big man's fists were like the hoofs of a mule. Claydon stumbled back. For a moment he swung the pistol blindly before him and drove his antagonist toward the hut. Then Krudenier came at him again, his long arms reaching for a hold. Claydon threw the pistol into his face, and saw blood spring out where the pistol sight ripped open the skin. Then Krudenier was back again, and his fists sank into Claydon's middle, but Claydon wasn't all fat. Claydon hit him twice in the crotch, stamped on his instep, and brought both fists down on the back of the man's neck when he bent over.

Krudenier fell on Claydon's feet. He rolled, his arms locked around the legs of Claydon, whose two hundred and forty pounds hit the hard ground with a jar. He twisted, came up face to face with Krudenier, and lunged at him, but the man rolled again, and Claydon went on his stomach. Krudenier leaped to his feet and kicked Claydon under the chin. The latter went back, spreadeagled for an instant, and the Frenchman was after him; but Claydon evaded him and got to his knees. Krudenier kicked him in the ear and battered him on the back of the head with his heavy fists. Claydon swayed on his knees, trying to get to his feet, but Krudenier jumped on his kidneys. Both men fell to the ground.

Claydon came up, breathing hard and trying to straighten his back, but Krudenier was on him, wrestling him to the ground and setting his teeth in Claydon's ear. Claydon jabbed at his eyes, and Krudenier jerked, taking part of the ear. Claydon, hunting the other's throat, felt blood on the Frenchman's chest, and knew for the first time approximately where the bullet had struck. He held his middle finger rigid, jabbing for the bullet hole. He found it, jabbed, and something gave. Krudenier drew up in a spasm of pain. Claydon leaped to his feet. The Frenchman was getting up slowly, his mouth open, his eyes glazed, when Claydon jumped at his matted face with both feet. Krudenier tried to hold his legs, but Claydon tore free. He butted the man in the face with his knees. Then he got a stranglehold, and Krudenier could not shake it off.

Claydon held on a long time, then gave the body a final shake, held it a moment, and dropped it into the cane.

He straightened up slowly, wiping the sweat off his forehead with the back of his hand. He stood for a moment, getting his bearings. Then he started toward the hut, breathing hard.

He stood just outside the doorway and looked down at the Osage girl. Her eyes were large in the dark. "*Wathisko tonga don-he,*" she murmured in a voice of awe. "You are a great man, and very strong."

As Claydon moistened his lips and stepped down to face her, something hit him in the back like a hurtling log. He was knocked forward against the girl, and for an instant his hands were on her bare waist, then he was over her like a cat and had turned to face the door with his knife in his hand.

He recognized Gómez' laugh. "You were big fool to

225

think he wouldn't know what was in your mind."

Claydon tried to locate the voice. "You followed Krudenier," he said.

Gómez seemed to be standing at one side of the door. "*Naturalmente.* I told you he had a weakness."

"You didn't help him out," Claydon said accusingly.

Gómez answered in the dark. "You make another big mistake. You don' worry about what I think."

Claydon moved two steps to one side.

Gómez said, "The squaw, she looks *simpatica* to me too—*bastante simpatica, amigo.*"

Claydon was creeping forward in the darkness of the hut on the balls of his feet. Suddenly he launched himself at the voice, striking hard with the knife. But he came face to face with the cottonwood door, and his knife sank into the soft wood. Then Gómez was at his back, the steel of his knife scraping Claydon's collarbone like a hot branding iron. Claydon wheeled and struck out, but Gómez backed away too fast for him. Claydon spun back to get his knife out of the spongy wood, but a flash of yellow fire filled the little room, and a hot ball of lead slammed into Claydon's thigh. Claydon turned back, balancing carefully to keep his leg from collapsing. He turned on his good leg, still hunting the sound of the voice.

Gómez said: "I do not like to do that, *amigo.* It brings dirt down from the roof, and besides, it scares the rats."

Claydon snarled and leaped, hitting the halfbreed in the chest with his fist. Then his leg gave way without warning. He went down, and Gómez jammed his second pistol against his ear. "If you are very quiet, *amigo,* I do not pull this trigger."

Claydon subsided. His back was sticky from the blood of the knife cuts, and his leg felt numb from the

226

hip down. "Nikaakibuno," Gómez ordered. *"Pe-dse."*

Claydon heard her soft steps across the dirt floor. He heard her blowing, and a fire began to glow in the hut. It became brighter, but Claydon's back was toward the fire. She must have fed some twigs into it, for it flared up suddenly. Claydon looked up at Gómez, lanky, cinnamon-colored, hook-nosed.

"We-thin," Gómez ordered the Osage girl.

Staying beyond Claydon's sight, she handed the halfbreed a long strip of rawhide.

Gómez prodded Claydon with his pistol. "On your stomach." Claydon rolled over painfully. Gómez tied his wrists with great care, and then dragged him to the fire and turned him on his back again.

"Ever since you make that strange remark about the guts around your legs, I have been want' to see how it is done," Gómez said. "When I finish, if you are not too uncomfortable, you will find the path to the river easy enough in the moonlight." He stopped to listen. "You hear? El Señor Lagarto bellows already. Maybe he is mad about the empty jug. Maybe he is want' a mate. Maybe he is hungry." He touched the edge of his knife with his thumb. "You think so?"

EPILOGUE

From *The Natchitoches Courier* of Monday, October 16, 1826:

VISTOR FROM KENTUCKY—AN INTERESTING EVENT occurred at a local Protestant church yesterday. Obadiah Price, a young farmer from the Kiamichi country up on the Red River, and his wife brought their six-month-old son and presented it for baptism. The child's grandparents, Nathan and Sarah Price, were in attendance—Nathan being a man of considerable substance, with a large farm northeast of Natchitoches. The little ceremony was also observed by the *great-grandmother,* a Mrs. Matthew Foley, who came from Kentucky for the occasion. The old lady is said to own a large amount of property, at the Falls of the Ohio, and is remarkably well preserved for a *great-grandmother.* She says she owes her good health and appearance to the salubriousness of the climate of the Western Country.

We hope that you enjoyed reading this
Sagebrush Large Print Western.
If you would like to read more Sagebrush titles,
ask your librarian or contact the Publishers:

United States and Canada

Thomas T. Beeler, *Publisher*
Post Office Box 659
Hampton Falls, New Hampshire 03844-0659
(800) 818-7574

United Kingdom, Eire, and
the Republic of South Africa

Isis Publishing Ltd
7 Centremead
Osney Mead
Oxford OX2 0ES England
(01865) 250333

Australia and New Zealand

Bolinda Publishing Pty. Ltd.
17 Mohr Street
Tullamarine, 3043, Victoria, Australia
(016103) 9338 0666